MW01148293

THE PRETENDING PLOT

LAUREN BLAKELY

ALSO BY LAUREN BLAKELY

Big Rock Series

Big Rock

Mister O

Well Hung

Full Package

Joy Ride

Hard Wood

The Gift Series

The Engagement Gift

The Virgin Gift

The Decadent Gift (coming soon)

The Heartbreakers Series

Once Upon a Real Good Time

Once Upon a Sure Thing

Once Upon a Wild Fling

Boyfriend Material

Asking For a Friend

Sex and Other Shiny Objects

One Night Stand-In

Lucky In Love Series

Most Valuable Playboy

Most Likely to Score

Standalones

Stud Finder

The V Card

The Real Deal

Unbreak My Heart

The Break-Up Album

21 Stolen Kisses

Out of Bounds

The Caught Up in Love Series:

The Swoony New Reboot of the Contemporary Romance Series

The Pretending Plot (previously called *Pretending He's Mine*)

The Dating Proposal

The Second Chance Plan (previously called *Caught Up In Us*)

The Private Rehearsal (previously called *Playing With Her Heart*)

Stars In Their Eyes Duet

My Charming Rival

My Sexy Rival

The No Regrets Series

The Thrill of It

The Start of Us

Every Second With You

The Seductive Nights Series

First Night (Julia and Clay, prequel novella)

Night After Night (Julia and Clay, book one)

After This Night (Julia and Clay, book two)

One More Night (Julia and Clay, book three)

A Wildly Seductive Night (Julia and Clay novella, book 3.5)

The Joy Delivered Duet

Nights With Him (A standalone novel about Michelle and Jack)

Forbidden Nights (A standalone novel about Nate and Casey)

The Sinful Nights Series

Sweet Sinful Nights

Sinful Desire

Sinful Longing

Sinful Love

The Fighting Fire Series

Burn For Me (Smith and Jamie)

Melt for Him (Megan and Becker)

Consumed By You (Travis and Cara)

The Jewel Series

A two-book sexy contemporary romance series

The Sapphire Affair

The Sapphire Heist

ABOUT

A delicious and all-new reimagining of Lauren Blakely's original fake fiancé romance!

I don't mean to just blurt it out. "Why, yes, I'm engaged!"

But once I say it to a potential client, there's only one logical thing to do—cast the role of my fake fiancé.

Easy enough. As a casting director, my job is to find the most talented players for every part, so I choose dreamy, edgy, sexy, sarcastic Reeve.

And I sign him up for one week in the role of mine.

It's not as if I'll fall for him in five nights even if we get a little cozy one night at the theater. It's not as if I'll want more even after a scorching afternoon in the stacks of the New York Public Library.

I can't let myself fall because on Friday at midnight the curtain drops on our fake romance . . .

The Pretending Plot is a reimagining of Pretending He's Mine, rewritten in first person, and expanded from a novella to novel length!

THE PRETENDING PLOT

By Lauren Blakely

Want to be the first to learn of sales, new releases, preorders and special freebies? Sign up for my VIP mailing list here!

AUTHOR'S NOTE

Dear Reader,

The Pretending Plot is a reimagining of the 2013 story Pretending He's Mine (no longer available for sale). The Pretending Plot has been rewritten in first person and expanded from a novella to novel length! I hope you enjoy this new tale for these characters!

Also, if you're curious, the events in THE PRETENDING PLOT take place concurrently with the events in THE SECOND CHANCE PLAN.

xoxo
Lauren

HIS PROLOGUE

Reeve

Present Day

The handcuffs snapped closed. I tugged, but all I got were red marks on my wrist. I could honestly say, I never thought I'd be in this position.

I'm not saying I never fantasized about being handcuffed by a beautiful woman while wearing only boxer briefs and cowboy boots. It was just that I wasn't a cowboy boots kind of guy.

"Tell me when it hurts," cooed a throaty voice.

"Doesn't hurt," I said.

A pair of hands slid around me, tugging on each end of the handcuffs. Another pair of hands skimmed up my back and I sucked in a breath. Sutton's hands. I recognized the feel of them instantly. Damn, she felt spectacular. Even though I wanted to be the one cuffing, the one calling the shots.

But then, striking this deal with Sutton Brenner had never been about calling the shots. It started and ended with her, with her glorious legs, her ice-blue eyes, her curtains of brown, silky hair, and a body I craved. And her hands. The ones tracing long, lingering lines up my back.

True, there were more than the three of us in the room, but I kept my head down and my eyes off of anyone else.

Sutton took her hands off me, and I focused on the moment.

"How about a cowboy hat before I take you for a ride?" asked the woman who'd handcuffed me.

I heard the crack of a whip against a palm, and then a wide-brimmed hat came down on my head, pushing my hair into my eyes. I couldn't see much, but I was sure Sutton was still here. I knew she thought her job was done. But we were just getting started.

Showtime.

HER PROLOGUE

Sutton

I'd seen a lot of young men with their shirts off. A fair number without their trousers too. I had an eye for the finest specimens, was an unapologetic aficionado of toned, muscled, and mouth-watering male flesh. I was not in the habit of sampling, however. I was like a sommelier, with an exhaustive understanding of vintage and an unfailing instinct for delicious pairings.

Which was to say, I knew how to pick 'em.

Reeve wasn't the typical rippling 200 pounds of muscle you'd see in a fireman's calendar, oiled and buffed to a high-gloss shine. He was anything but the standard-order bachelorette-party beefcake with a bow tie and a big smile. There was something a bit more refined about him. He was a Renaissance masterwork—not only those cheekbones, but his body, as well. He was longer, lankier, with the tightly toned frame of a cyclist, but filled out in all the right places. Trim waist, cut abs, arms with just the right amount of definition. And that hair, so soft and inviting.

I bit my lip, cataloguing each time I'd run my fingers through that hair. There was that night . . . Oh, and *that* day—that had been a very good day. Because, sure, he was chained to a bedpost *now*, but fair was fair when it came to objectification. I'd taken my turn, and I grinned privately, adding to my catalogue all the times he'd had his way with me.

But *this* moment was about him. About him and the spotlight and the bargain we'd struck five months ago.

1

REEVE

Five Months Ago

Callback.

The word whispered promises, spun out fantasies of hope and possibility. After an audition, there was no word an actor wanted to hear more than that.

But hell if it wasn't a big tease. It was the rabbit at the greyhound track, the classy AF woman in a bar full of dude-bros, the tantalizing carrot tied at the end of the just-longer-than-your-reach stick.

I'd gotten the word on my voice mail, in my email. There were showers and droughts, and lately it was the Mojave Desert. I hadn't gotten one callback since I finished the run of an off-Broadway production of *Les Mis*. The producers had modernized the show so I had gotten to sing like a rock star, and I felt like one too, earning comparisons by critics to the lead singer of Arcade Fire in one review, and Muse in another.

The show closed a few weeks ago, and I found myself where young actors in New York often find themselves. Looking for a job. It was a constant state as a thespian. You had to live your life on the edge of want every single day. If there was anything else I remotely wanted to do with my life—be a cop like my dad, or a high school English teacher, like my mom, I'd have signed up for the police academy or a teaching degree a few years ago. But acting was my passion, the thing I couldn't live without, and so, at age twenty-four, I'd amassed some decent credits, and a few nice gigs, but not a ton of dough. Despite the reviews for *Les Mis*, I'd only made a few thousand bucks from the show.

That was the problem with theater. It barely satisfied the beast of New York City rent.

Sure, there were commercials, and I had snagged a couple spots, pimping whitening toothpaste in one, and flashing my bright, perfect smile. Hey, I don't mean to brag. Thank the years of braces as a kid. But I needed a bigger payday. If I could nab a meaty role in a film or land a part in a breakout TV show, I'd be done strapping on a messenger bag and zipping through traffic like I had a death wish. Bike messengers were still in demand by law offices and financial firms, but the clients could be douchebags, and I got tired of the dirty looks from pinstriped-suited men in elevators. As if they'd never seen a guy with bike grease on his cheeks before.

Today was one of those days. A snooty lady in an office building had made me take the stairs fifteen flights rather than the elevator, then I'd been nearly clipped by a cab making an illegal turn on Third Avenue, and to top it off I'd almost gotten sideswiped by a bus when the driver didn't bother to look whether the lane was clear. Was it so much to ask for drivers to pay attention?

Now, I was racing against the clock to deliver documents for a deal closing.

"Hold the door," I called out as the brass elevator doors of a swank Park Avenue office building started to shut. The whole place was gold-plated and marble-floored and reeked of insanely high hourly billing rates, the likes of which I could barely even imagine.

I ran over to the lift, messenger bag smacking the back of my T-shirt, and raced inside. The gray-haired man who'd held the door gave me a quick once-over and then snorted a "harrumph" and shook his head.

"Need a tissue? Some cough drops, maybe?" I asked, because I knew the blue blood was dissing me in my streetwear, my bike helmet still on and finger-less gloves on my hands, and the attitude ticked me off.

"Shouldn't you be taking the service elevator, young man?"

"Oh, right. I should," I muttered under my breath while staring at the elevator buttons. "Because I might infect the people in here with my low-paying, grubby, barely-covers-the-rent job."

Evidently, the man had good hearing. "I could call building security on you."

Crap. The guy probably owned the building. I should have known better. I should have shut my mouth. I should have said, "Yes sir, I will take that elevator next time." But honestly, the whole bike-messenger-in-the-service-elevator was supposed to be a thing of the past.

"Sorry," I said.

We stepped out on the same floor and walked into a glass-paneled office suite.

"Hello, Mr. Fitzpatrick," the receptionist said, and I cringed as I handed her the package. "For Mr. Fitz-patrick," I said in a low voice.

I turned tail, ready to get the hell out of the office, when Mr. Fitzpatrick called out to the receptionist. "Sally, dear. Would you please look into a new messenger service for our documents?"

Fuck. My boss was going to skewer me. Why did I have to make a snide comment? I didn't usually let pointed remarks get the better of me. But it wasn't even the Richie-Rich dude in the suit I was pissed at. I was still pissed at myself over blowing a callback a few weeks ago.

It had been a plum role. A supporting part in a new Joss Whedon flick. I'd nailed the first audition, then I'd prepped and practiced my lines over and over before the callback. That was the problem. I'd wrung all the feelings from the words after one too many solo rehearsals in front of the bathroom mirror. By the time I opened my mouth for the camera, I was on autopilot. I knew from the way the producer had said "Thanks, we'll be in touch" that I'd flubbed it, and I only had myself to blame.

Now, I'd lost a client for Swift as Light.

I left the Park Avenue building, spotting the flashing red light on my phone. My boss had probably called to ream me out. There was a text message too. *What the hell did you do???* I ignored it, unlocked my bike, and hopped into the saddle, speed-demoning it down the traffic-infested streets of New York, spewing a stream of curse words as I gripped the handlebars. Now I'd have to give my best mea culpa to my boss at the Swift as Light offices in the East Village. When I arrived, I wheeled my bike inside, parked it in the cluttered hallway, and found Dave waiting for me. Hands on hips. Bearded face lined with anger. "What the hell was that about? Swift as Light is finito. History. Gone."

I pulled the messenger bag over my head and dropped it on the floor. "Sorry."

He arched an angry brow. Wait, make that a mad-as-a-wild-boar brow. "You're sorry? That's what you have to say? That was an important client, and it's not like the bike messenger business has to compete with, oh, you know, DoorDash, and GrubHub, and a million new other services every damn day. I don't have the luxury of losing clients when you're pissed."

My shoulders tightened, and guilt swirled in me. I repeated, more sincerely, "I'm sorry."

He huffed, waving a hand, his dark eyes brooking no argument. "What the fuck is wrong with you? Don't fucking talk to people. Just keep your mouth shut."

"Look, I almost got killed out there. Drivers are assholes. I'm having a shit day."

"Welcome to being an adult. Every day can be a shit day. You don't have to be a dick to the clients."

"I didn't know he was a client," I said, then instantly hated myself for sounding defensive. I'd fucked up, plain and simple. There was no real excuse.

"Assume everyone is. Got that? Assume everyone is a client and shut your mouth. You're not in a Tarantino film. You're in a job. So act like it."

"Okay. Got the message." I held up my hands, as if surrendering.

"And go take a week off to cool down."

"What?" My jaw dropped. Was he for real?

And the answer was yes. "I gotta spend the day trying to triage this and figure out if I can save a client. If I see you around, it'll piss me off. So get out of here and come back in a week. We'll see if I no longer want to strangle you with one of your dumbass T-shirts with their stupid sayings," Dave said, and walked back into his office in a trail of annoyance.

I glanced down at my well-worn blue T-shirt, heaving a sigh. Now my T-shirts were to blame too? What was wrong with my T-shirts? This one had the words "Beehives are not piñatas" in a cool font across the front. The shirt looked good on me. Some chick at the corner bodega where I got my morning coffee had even said "cool shirt." I could rock a worn T-shirt like nobody's business thanks to my lean and muscular frame.

Gyms were my friends. No excuses as an actor. You just went.

And today, I went away from work, frustrated with myself.

I snagged my bike, left the office, and called Jill. We'd been friends for a while but became even tighter when we were in *Les Mis* together. Tight in the close friends kind of way. Tight in the way a dude can be buddies with a chick.

"Come on over tonight and we'll drown your sorrows," she said. "My roommate's visiting her parents so we can be as loud and obnoxious as we want."

"Because if she were here, you'd be quiet and considerate?" I teased.

"As if I'm capable of that."

"I'll be over after seven. I'm going to the gym. I have to blow off some steam."

"Good. Because you are not permitted to come over angry. It would totally ruin my Feng Shui crystal healing energy vibe."

I laughed. "Since when are you into new age stuff?"

"Since never. But I got something nice from a marathon mommy and it's got your name written all over it."

"Can't wait to see what it is. See you later, babe."

After a stint at the gym and a quick shower, I walked across town to Jill's apartment in Chelsea and she buzzed me up.

"I have beer and vodka. Pick your poison." Jill waggled a long-neck bottle in one hand, and a short glass with ice cubes and clear liquid in the other.

"Vodka," I said and took a long swallow of the liquor, downing most of the drink.

"Whoa, Tiger. Slow it down."

I just shrugged, thrust the glass at Jill, and affixed my best commercial toothpaste smile. "May I have another, pretty please?"

"Fine," she said, pouring more into the glass.

I eyed the fancy bottle. "Since when do you buy Belvedere?"

"This is the *something nice* I got. It was a gift from one of the ladies in my running club who finished the New York City marathon."

"She gave you vodka for finishing a marathon? Correct me if I'm wrong, but isn't that sort of counter to the whole marathon vibe?"

She grinned. "Vodka and marathons are like headliners and featured cast—they go together great as long as you remember who comes first. And I genuflected at her gift, because I love my Belvedere almost as much as I adore Sondheim. Now, come to my couch, and tell me all your problems," she said, pointing to the mustard-colored couch, well-worn from many late-night talk sessions.

I glanced around, seeing signs of Kat, in the Eiffel Tower and Arc de Triomphe mugs on the kitchen shelf and a couple of French Provincial type prints mixed in the decor. "So, your roomie's in Paris?"

"She's on a mission to find new designs for her necklaces. I'm excited for her. Also, she's got this complicated love life thing going on." She sipped her drink. "Who knows how that will turn out, but I want the best for her."

"Yeah, I can tell by the way you keep poking your nose in her love life. Caden told me you steered them together at the opening night party."

Jill waved a hand in the air, dismissing her interference. "Some people need steering. Especially roommates who are hung up on guys they should not be hung up on." Then she slid a sly glance at me. "And guy friends who should be making some woman deliriously happy with his triple threat of looks, talent, and niceness."

I put up my hands to hold her off, metaphorically. "What about my triple threat of jobless, penniless, and auditionless? I am in a first-things-first holding pattern where romance is concerned."

"Wait—jobless?" She made a sad face, bottom lip stuck out in a pout. "When did this happen?" Uncurling from the corner of the couch, she put her feet on the coffee table and motioned me toward her with open arms. "Come tell Auntie Jill all about it and we'll figure it out."

With a groan in the same vein as her exaggerated but sincere sympathy, I stretched out on the couch and rested my head in Jill's lap. She ran her fingers through my hair. It was comforting and comfortable, but familial like a sibling. Actors are naturally touchy people. We are used to having hands on each other, whether on stage or in rehearsals, so it becomes a natural state of affairs when hanging out.

"Let's see. Well, I totally fucked up my audition for

the Joss Whedon film, as you know. Second, I haven't booked a commercial in weeks. Third, I'm pretty sure the residuals from my last toothpaste spot are going to dry up soon. Fourth, my boss at the messenger service is forcing me to take a week off without pay because I was rude"—I sketched air quotes around the word—"to one of my customers."

"Ouch." She shot me a sympathetic look. "Were you, though?"

I drew a deep breath, taking this one on the chin since I deserved it. "I was a dick. I deserve the week of no pay. Which brings me to the fifth problem. Rent. Rent. Rent."

Jill stared pensively at a cracked section of plaster on the ceiling. "You know, Reeve," she said, in a voice that I instantly recognized as her mastermind tone. "One of the Upper East Side cougars in my running club has a high-end escort service going on."

I laughed and sat up straight. "Seriously? You want me to be an escort?"

She gestured broadly to my frame, like she was saying I could play the part. "Is it such a crazy thought? You're young and hot and you can play any part. That's what these ladies want."

"What kind of ladies?" I asked, intrigued, if only because it was intriguing as fuck.

"All kinds," Jill said, in an evasive way.

Now I had to know. "What do you mean all kinds?"

She shrugged sheepishly. "Just that all sorts of ladies use escort services."

"Do you?"

She swatted me with a pillow. "No!"

"Just saying you can admit it if you do."

She rolled her eyes. "And to think I was trying to help you with a job."

"And to think you have a client in your running club who's a pimp," I said and pushed my fingers through my hair.

"She's not a pimp, Reeve," Jill said, correcting, as she punched me on the shoulder. "She's a high-end madam. For men. And she pays well."

That's what I needed more than anything. Dough. Plain and simple. But escort work? I don't know. That wasn't my style. Even so, I was curious about what was entailed. "Would I have to, you know, with them?"

"Go down on them?"

I made a rolling motion with my hand. "That and other things."

Jill shrugged. "Probably in some cases. I mean, some women just read Playgirl for the articles, but I'm pretty sure when you're shelling out a thousand dollars a pop you want the escort to take care of the lady business."

"A thousand dollars a pop?" That was eye-popping money.

"Too much? You don't feel right charging that? Don't worry. I can tell her you'd be willing to work at a discount," she teased, deadpan.

And the thing was—the money was as appealing as anything.

But the work was not.

I had no interest in providing those kinds of services. I wasn't old-fashioned, but maybe in some ways, I was. "I think I'll keep looking for work. Call me crazy, but I kind of like actually—you know—being attracted to the girl I'm making scream my name out loud."

"Do you, Reeve? Do you make them scream your name out loud?"

I raised an eyebrow playfully. "Every. Single. Time."

I'd checked the mirror on the way out the door that morning and made sure I didn't *look* like a woman with everything on the line.

Poised on the cusp of a life-changing opportunity —that was what I wanted to project. Today I needed to lock down a contract that any of my competitors would walk on hot coals to get. But I was the right one—the only one—for this project. I had been prepping for this most of my career.

Escorted Lives.

The red-hot film based on the biggest selling erotic romance series the world had seen in ages.

Who had better credentials when it came to redhot and sexy? Who cast *It's Raining Men*, the blockbuster male stripper movie which had showered $302 million in box-office greenbacks onto the producers?

Sutton Brenner, that's the one.

And then there was *Spread*, an indie flick about a chiseled male model who falls in love with an Oklahoma housewife. That festival darling was my break-out, earning both critical acclaim and a cool one hundred twelve million, ten times its budget. And *I* earned a nod in an industry trade magazine, touted as "the best appraiser of male flesh and talent in all of the film community."

I'd been tickled pink by the accolade.

But it wasn't ink on a contract.

The money guys on *Escorted Lives* hadn't yet committed to signing me to cast their film. In my mirror pep talk, I told myself they were being cautious. I had an excellent track record, but at twenty-eight, it was a relatively short one. But if I were honest with the woman in the mirror, I'd admit that mega-rich Johnathan and Nicholas Pinkerton were known in the business as risk-takers.

So that's where we were figuratively—the edge of the high dive, waiting for the whistle to say "go."

Literally, I was perched on the edge of my chair across the glass conference table from the twin British film financiers. They were my countrymen, and I hoped that my own Britishness might give me a leg up. I could—and did—talk the talk about London and the Queen and footie, and they loved that. They were avid golfers too, and so I'd researched the blazes out of golf in America so I could chat them up about the relative merits of the Augusta National Club versus Pebble Beach Golf Links, and, please God, they'd never guess I didn't know a lick about swinging a club.

Would my prep work pay off?

"You're definitely at the top of the list for *Escorted Lives*," Johnathan said. I waited for, *so of course we're going with you,* but the producer trailed off.

Bollocks.

Top of the list meant there was still a list. What was the holdup?

As if I'd asked the question aloud, Johnathan glanced at his wife, Janelle. She'd been silent through the meeting so far—the obvious sort of silence that speaks loudly—with her hands folded on the table and her lips pressed tightly together.

It was not a good sign. If the Pinkerton brothers were famously known as risk-takers, then the Pinkerton Power Couple was *in*famously mercurial, with a stormy marriage that bled over—or so it was rumored—into their business and social lives.

My role centered around appearances—not physical beauty (my reputation in the subset of handsome male actors aside), but rather the story that a person's appearance told—or *could* tell—with guidance from the right director.

Janelle's green eyes were cool and piercing. Her black hair was pulled back in a bun so tight that her skin looked stretched over her scalp. Her perfect makeup and her straight, still posture reminded me of a doll—the kind meant to be displayed on a shelf, not played with on the floor.

Janelle wasn't the toy, but the puppeteer. I hadn't only researched golf courses. Gathering intel on the Pinkertons was simplicity itself. Janelle was the money—she came from it and Johnathan married into it. She might not have the official title of executive producer, but everything in a Johnathan Pinkerton movie had to pass muster with the wife. That was hardly a secret.

After that, it was a matter of sorting credible rumor from wild speculation. Opinions were split on whether she held the purse strings in an iron fist or one that tightened or slackened depending on the current state of their turbulent marriage.

And Johnathan Pinkerton had recently been featured in a gossip tabloid photo, looking very cozy with the not-so-wide-eyed ingenue in his previous production.

This could be bad.

While I'd been trying not to stare at Janelle, she'd been less subtle about looking me over. My mirror pep-talk had been to an attractive, one might even say *sexy* if one weren't too British to admit it aloud, well-put-together and not-at-all-desperate-looking woman perhaps fifteen years younger than Mrs. Pinkerton.

This could be very bad, indeed.

Finally, she moved, leaning closer to Johnathan and whispering something in his ear. They then had an exchange that seemed as much significant glares and knowing looks as actual words. Which I might have had a chance of interpreting if Nicholas Pinkerton hadn't filled the awkward silence by making conversation about bloody golf.

I smiled and nodded until Johnathan Pinkerton cleared his throat, reclaiming the meeting.

"As I was saying, we think your previous work makes you suited for this project. We like to promote a familial sort of culture at Pinkerton, and thought perhaps you would like to join us for a dinner party on Friday." Janelle cleared her throat, and Johnathan's smile tightened. "And your fiancé, of course."

"Come again?" I asked, unsure I'd heard him correctly.

Because I didn't *have* a fiancé.

Johnathan's brows knitted. "I was sure I'd read in the papers you were recently engaged."

I blinked—fortunately I'd held my emotional cards close and my face pleasantly neutral.

The papers. An engagement. *Of course.*

I saw exactly how the mistake came about. The Broadway actress Sutton Kenmore had become engaged to her manager last week. There weren't many Suttons in New York or in show biz, so this was far from the first time someone had gotten some detail turned around in their head.

I was about to explain that there'd been a misunderstanding, but Janelle piped up. "We *do* so love to meet the significant people in the lives of our team. A dinner gathering will be just the opportunity to finalize the details." She gave an arch look at my bare left hand. "And perhaps show off your ring . . .?"

Ah-ha! There it was. The click of the pieces coming together—the tabloid photo, the pencil skirt and heels I'd carefully chosen this morning, the *familial culture* I had heard nothing of until that whispered conversation—it all translated to "no unattached women attached to this project."

Quickly, I weighed my options. The obvious choice—straighten out the confusion, laugh it off, and move on.

But we *weren't* moving at all on this deal. This meeting was the first movement in weeks, and the only thing to have changed was this "engagement." It was difficult not to attribute cause and effect.

And beyond that—I could read people and I could read between the lines too. They wanted me to be attached.

I knew a lucky break when I saw it. I was the best person to cast this film whether I was single, married, or celibate. My relationship status said nothing of my skills.

But my skills also said that sometimes you need to seize the chance. To make someone else's biases work to your benefit. If they needed an attached woman, they'd get an attached woman, and I'd deliver a terrific film, dust my hands, and move on.

You don't let a golden opportunity pass you by.

Improvising, I held up my ringless hand. "My boyfriend surprised me the other weekend. The ring is being resized. I can't wait to get it back on my hand." I gave it all the gleeful enthusiasm a recently betrothed twenty-eight-year-old casting director might feel. And really, wasn't I all but one of those things? The remaining thing mattered not in the long run.

Not one damn bit.

"Then it's all settled," Janelle said. She'd even thawed enough to smile without cracking her face. "We can't wait to have dinner with you and your fiancé on Friday night."

"Yes," I echoed, wondering how the not-looking-ruffled thing was going now. "All settled."

But woman does not survive by her wits alone. I needed reinforcements for this dilemma and fired off a text to my friend McKenna in California.

Sutton: Mayday! I have 4 days to get engaged.

McKenna: Is that the title of a new Rom-Com you're casting? Because it sounds like the premise of one.

Sutton: If only. I have to produce a fiancé by Friday night if I want to score this job on the new Pinkerton movie.

McKenna: omg! Are you casting *Entangled Lives? Escorted Lives?* Which was the first book? It doesn't matter. You have to work on it, and you have to tell me who's going to be in it.

Sutton: The answer to all those questions is I DON'T KNOW. Because I have to have a fiancé, but I DON'T have a fiancé, and the queue to take my place goes

around the block. This movie is the hottest thing
going on in the casting world right now. Everyone
wants in on it. Especially every good-looking young
actor in—well, on either coast. And some on other
continents.

McKenna: It seems like you have your ANSWER
right there. This is what you DO, WOMAN. You are
the Duchess of Beefcake. You are the Ace of Eye-
candy. How many hot firemen have you cast?

Sutton: A lot.

McKenna: Tattooed Bad Boys, All-American athletes .
. . Stop me when I get to one that appeals to you.

Sutton: You're saying I should cast the role of my
fiancé?

McKenna: Well, the closest thing you have to a man
in your life is your dog. You could hire an escort
service, but that might be a little meta for the East
Coast.

Sutton: I don't know. Mrs. Pinkerton is eagle-eyed.
I'd say she's paranoid about her husband's wandering
eye. For me to pull off this farce of a fiancé, I need a
man who is truly my type. Someone I can realistically
be in a relationship with.

McKenna: Tell me again how many hard-bodied, 8-

pack packing men you auditioned for *It's Raining Men*?

Sutton: Yes, it's a tough job I have. But in all seriousness, that movie called for stripper types, beefcake, and bravado. I had never gone for those kinds of guys. This job needs less swagger. More finesse.

McKenna: Then you can guess my next question. What IS your type?

Sutton: You have to swear not to laugh.

McKenna: This is a text message. You can't tell if I'm laughing.

Sutton: I beg to differ. I will absolutely be able to tell. So . . . you have been warned. Truth be told, I'd always had a thing for hipsters. A little bit of stubble, a little bit of attitude, a tattoo on the arm, slim but not too skinny jeans that show off his assets. Sexy, but with a touch of innocence to him.

McKenna: Mmm . . . That's a tall order. Everyone underrates vulnerability in a guy. Someone still willing to believe in Santa Claus and the Easter Bunny. I mean, metaphorically. Not like Will Farrell in *Elf* type belief.

Sutton: But that was endearing, right? Only it was played for broad comedy because of course being vulnerable, being fresh, would wring all the masculinity from a man like a tea towel. But picture the wide-eyed wonder a superhero has when he first learns he has special powers. Oh!

McKenna: Was that a good 'Oh' or a bad one?

Sutton: I just thought of someone. I'm sending you his headshot.

McKenna: Whoa. Also, you just have his picture lying around?

Sutton: Of course not. The only picture on my desk is of The Artful Dodger's adorable brown sweet silky face. But I have a folder with the vital info on everyone who's ever auditioned for me.

McKenna: Nice work if you can get it.

Sutton: If you think I'm going to disagree with you, you're wrong. But I've never regretted calling this fellow in for any audition. He was witty, clever, and frankly, irresistible. A bit of the boy toy about him. Every, ahem, slightly older woman's dream.

McKenna: ohmygod, Sutton. Twenty-eight is too young to be a cougar.

Sutton: Did I say cougar? I believe YOU did, love

McKenna: So cheeky. And yes, I did. Owning it! Tell me about your boy toy.

Sutton: He's adorable, but he has that chased-with-danger look in his eyes.

McKenna: That look is perfect for you. Just one thing —I thought you never dated actors.

Sutton: And I still won't have dated one.

McKenna: Right. Just have been fake-engaged to one.

Sutton: But that's why this is such a great idea! There's no chance that I could truly fall for him because I have less than no romantic interest in an actor. I'd have a built-in safety net. We'd both simply be trying to get a job.

McKenna: You know . . . if you went out for more than walks with The Artful Dodger, you might meet someone who could be a real boyfriend. Crazy idea, right?

Sutton: Absolutely barking mad, that idea. And on that note, it's noon on Monday, and I have to be engaged by Friday, so I'd better get cracking.

3

REEVE

That was a beleaguered sigh if I ever heard one.

The sigher in question put some money down to cover his tab and picked up his phone and his ballcap from the bar I'd been tending. "Thanks for the beer, man, and for listening."

"Anytime," I said. "Good luck."

After the heave-ho from Dave, I'd called around to friends and acquaintances, putting out the word that I was hoping to pick up some shifts bartending. I wasn't one to sit on my ass waiting for another toothpaste commercial to drop in my lap. And I was good at it—bartending, not ass-sitting—as an actor, I had plenty of practice.

I'd nabbed a shift at the Lucky Spot for Sunday evening, a Midtown joint owned by my friends Spencer and Charlotte.

"Thanks for helping out in a pinch," Spencer said, clapping me on the back.

"Thank you for throwing some work my way."

"Not a problem." He eyed the door, nodding to the customer who'd just left. "Keeping your life-coach skills sharp too, I see."

I shrugged it off. "Comes with the territory, right?"

He laughed. "If I had a nickel for all the relationship advice I've given . . ."

"You'd need a bigger piggybank."

"See? More excellent advice." He chuckled and left me to finish my shift.

The key, really, to customers thinking I was Dear Abby was to listen and nod while they talked their way around to their own answers. Fortunately, I was a people person.

Once I finished my shift, I cleaned up, locked up, and headed home. On the way, I checked my email for any notes from my agent.

There were none.

But there was always tomorrow.

* * *

And boom. Optimism paid off by lunchtime on Monday with an audition.

I punched a fist in the air when I hung up with my agent, who'd gotten a call from a casting director I'd worked with before. I'd tried out for *It's Raining Men*, and had returned for a second and third callback, but ultimately the bigger roles had gone to bigger names. That stung, getting that far but losing out on even a supporting role. I had snagged a day role, though, as a bartender at the strip club. Even that, in a block-buster, was a big fucking deal.

That was then.

Now the casting director wanted to see me, and my agent had sounded so enthusiastic I couldn't help but be fired up. Sutton Brenner, very British and very sexy, wanted me in her office in two hours.

I popped up from the couch in my cardboard-box–size apartment, dropped my phone onto the beat-up wooden coffee table, and changed into one of my favorite T-shirts, reviewing all the things I knew about Sutton Brenner as I brushed my teeth—the movies she'd cast, the shows she'd worked on . . . Then there were the personal details. She had a dog who was the center of her world, and I was pretty sure the dog had a strange name. As I capped the toothpaste, I remembered it.

So very British, indeed.

I grinned. Clever too.

I checked myself out in the cracked mirror on the closet door. Yep. I looked the way casting directors wanted me to look—young and dreamy, but with a bit of an edge. That was my type, and I had to lean into it. The kind of guy you could clean up with a short hair-cut, button-down shirt, and pants to bring home to mom and dad, but the same guy a girl would gladly slide in behind on a motorcycle for a ride to a secluded make-out spot. Those were the roles I knew I could win.

I left and headed for Sutton Brenner's Madison Avenue office, where the receptionist showed me in immediately. At the end of a long hallway, Sutton stood in the doorway, one hand on the door, the other on her waist, one long, tall drink of woman.

Holy hell, she was a smoke show.

If I'd met her under different circumstances, say, a bar or a club, I'd have walked straight up to her, asked her name, bought her a drink, and then charmed her. I imagined she could hold her own, giving as good as she got with witty banter that sounded even smarter and savvier in her oh-so-proper British accent. She'd have done that hair flip thing, all the more alluring with her thick brown tresses, then she'd have hooked me with those cool blue eyes. After I'd hailed a cab for her and given her a long, slow, lingering kiss by the curb, she'd have said, "Come home with me." I'd have done just that, and discovered whether she wore thigh-high stockings, as I always suspected. I'd have peeled them off her long, lean legs—peeled them off with my teeth.

What could I say? I knew what I liked, and oh hell, did I like her look. And did I lust for her accent.

But I wasn't here for ye olde libido.

I needed to focus on business, on work, on playing whatever part she required of me. I was sure none of those things involved removing her stockings, so I cleared her curves from my thoughts.

"Come in, Reeve," she said, and closed the door behind us, gesturing to her couch. I sat, doing my best to project coolness and confidence. Whatever Sutton was casting, I was sure those were vital character traits.

She sat in the chair opposite. Just for a moment, her short, black skirt rode up, and I glimpsed—accidentally, I swear—the lace tops of her thigh-high stockings, peeking out from below the hemline.

Oh, sweet mother of pearl.

Then she smoothed down her skirt in a natural, automatic movement that said short skirts were something she wore a lot. She also wore a white blouse with a few buttons undone, just enough for a peek of collarbone, which was somehow as hot as cleavage would be on someone else. Her hair was pinned up and her sexy glasses made me think "hot-for-teacher."

Settle down, libido.

"Good to see you again, Ms. Brenner," I said, going for the professional approach. Obviously.

She laughed lightly. "Call me Sutton, please."

I flashed a crooked smile. "Sutton it is, then. How's your dog? The Artful Dodger, right?" Good thing I'd remembered.

Sutton grinned brightly. "You remember."

"I think I do. Let's see . . . He's a little Chihuahua/Min Pin?"

"Yes!" It was as if I'd performed a magic trick at her birthday party, the way she smiled at me. "He is absolutely the love of my life. He's such a darling."

She didn't seem in a rush to get to business. Casting directors sometimes liked to get a read on an actor's own personality before they took on a character's. I considered it a good sign that whatever she had in mind meant spending time on set.

"And what does he do when you're at work?" I asked.

"Why, he goes to doggy daycare, of course. As if I would leave my darling alone all day." She sounded playful, which was something I couldn't say was common—not among casting directors or people in general. At least, it couldn't be common for someone to look so good while talking about her dog, and I selfishly kept her on the subject.

"Do they have a rigid agenda at doggy daycare? Peanut butter Kongs at ten, playtime and belly rubs at two?"

"Don't be silly. Belly rubs just before he has his tea, then playtime after."

"So, Mary Poppins works at this daycare?"

Now her laugh was rich and deep, less artful and more natural, like I'd taken her off guard. That laugh took me the same way.

"I'm so very glad I called you," she said, and that seemed as unplanned as her laugh.

"I am too." Then I scraped my hand over my jaw, feeling sheepish. "Though, I suppose that's stating the obvious."

"Is it?" she asked. Then she seemed to catch herself. "Ah yes. The job."

As much as I needed work, I hadn't meant it the way it had sounded, like I'd wanted to steer her back to business. So, I softened it up with a cheeky smile and a, "That too."

She flashed a quick smile, but seemed a bit more direct as she brushed her hands down her skirt. "Yes.

As you say, obviously I didn't ask you here to talk about my dog."

I shrugged. "It's nice to remember that people like you aren't actually fire-breathing dragons who feast nightly on flame-roasted actor for dinner."

"Not at all," she said, humor coming back into her voice. "Roast actor is really just for Sunday supper."

"And it's only Monday. So, lucky me."

How weird was it that I was trying to put the casting director at ease? I was anxious about work, but not about this meeting. It seemed like she knew what I brought to the table as an actor, and I'd either be right for the part or not.

With a decisive nod, she leaned forward, elbows on her knee, hands clasped loosely, classic "let's make a deal" pose.

"Reeve, I have a proposition for you."

My eyebrows climbed, and I knew my smile turned flirty in spite of myself. "I can't wait to hear it."

Lucky me, indeed.

4

SUTTON

This might work out better than I planned. Reeve was my type physically—strong and muscular, his jeans the best kind of tight. He worked out, but he didn't work out too much, and that was vital. Plus, he was quick with a quip and he liked four-legged friends. He was the ideal pretend boyfriend.

Perfect—I was attracted enough to pull this off. But I'd keep up my barriers, keep it all business. I was hiring him to play a part, after all. "This job is a bit unconventional. It's sort of a live theater type of role."

"Can't wait to hear about it," he said. He had a lovely voice—silky and melodic, the kind of voice that could sell you anything.

"It's also a part that's . . . how shall we say . . . off the books? Sort of a secret deal."

"Secrets make everything better," he said, with a playful wink. He waited for me to go on, but I was having an uncharacteristically hard time getting to the point of the meeting.

"Reeve, you know I've always found you incredibly attractive."

"Oh, yeah?" He took the compliment but seemed unsure where to put it.

I wasn't one to dance around when it came to offers, so I bit the bullet. "That's why I want you to pretend to be my boyfriend for a week."

He laughed, sounding shocked. "Why?"

"I have an opportunity to land a job I want badly, and it seems the producers were under the mistaken impression that I recently got engaged. Because, you know, Sutton Kenmore . . ." I said and made a rolling gesture, letting him fill in the rest. Reeve surely knew the other Sutton, or knew of her. She was one of the few theater actors with enough star wattage to open a Broadway show on her own.

He nodded. "Ah, Sutton Kenmore. She was in that *Oklahoma* revival last year, and she recently got hitched to her manager, I heard."

"Right. Exactly. Well, engaged, actually, and that's the thing—the Pinkertons made a point of emphasizing their family atmosphere. Janelle Pinkerton was rather pointed about it—how they're *so* looking forward to meeting my fiancé. So, well, I decided I should just go along with it."

Reeve smiled and shook his head in an admiring sort of way. "Clever."

"Only if I can pull it off. And that's why I called you. I want you to take on the role of my fiancé for a week."

He blinked, furrowed his brow. "So, *that's* the acting job you called me in for?"

"I'll pay you of course." I feared he might be disappointed that it wasn't an on-camera acting job, but the check would cash just the same.

He rubbed a hand across the back of his neck, like he was taking his time, absorbing all this intel. "What's the job you're trying to get?"

"It's for the film *Escorted Lives*," I said. Then I watched and waited as Reeve's delicious brown eyes lit up. His lips curved into a grin like he was anticipating a large haul of birthday presents this year.

No surprise. Every actor wanted in on this movie. Of course Reeve would too. I hadn't considered that it might sound as if I were suggesting some quid pro quo, and I hastened to clarify what I meant by payment.

"I'm prepared to offer you five thousand dollars," I said. "And of course, this is just for appearing in public as a couple. Not for any . . . funny business."

But he was already shaking his head. "I don't want money."

The way he captured my gaze didn't say: "I'm out." It said: "I want something else," and I held my breath waiting for his counteroffer.

5

REEVE

Escorted Lives was one of the bestselling books in the last few years. It started as a self-published novel and shot up the charts with its red-hot story of a woman who ran an escort service but also had her own particular sexual proclivities. After one too many episodes of cheating by her husband, she turned to voyeurism for her kicks and got off watching her stable of hot young men handle their lady clients. It had been jokingly referred to as the novel the world beat off to.

Funny that the other night, I'd told Jill I had no interest in being an escort for Upper East Side ladies. And here I was being offered something of a man-for-hire gig . . . to help Sutton Brenner get a contract to cast a movie about a man-for-hire gig.

"I'm prepared to offer you five thousand dollars," Sutton said, and the thought of the money made my heart beat a whole lot faster. I could use that dough. Oh hell, could I use it. But then I flashed back to my parents, to my dad who'd been a cop his whole life. To my mom, who taught high school English. My parents had a hard enough time accepting that I wanted to be an actor and make a go of it in New York City. But to take money for a fake boyfriend job?

Sutton had specifically said "no funny business," so she wasn't asking for anything salacious—other than putting on a con, I guess. But there was something I wanted more. And this was my moment to ask for it. Go big or go home.

Putting it all on the line, I met her gaze, gave my terms. "I don't want money. I want an audition for the producers and for the director. I want a chance to get the lead role."

I watched as she took a deep breath and considered my request. It was unconventional to bypass the casting director, but then, this deal was unconventional. Besides, it wasn't every day that I landed an opportunity like this. I would have liked the money, but I couldn't bring myself to take it. I wouldn't have felt right asking for a role outright, either. I wanted to be paid in the currency most valuable to me—opportunity. I had confidence I could parlay it into something good. I'd have a great audition. I planned to do everything differently from the Joss Whedon audition. I'd be as natural and I'd be as authentic as the producer could want.

Sutton didn't take long to answer, nodding a second or two later. "I'll get you an audition for them, Reeve," she said and flashed a smile, then winked. "How strange would it be if my fiancé—such a fine specimen at that—didn't get an audition, right? But if for some reason I don't nab the job, I will insist on paying you."

I waved a hand. I had enough faith in her talent for both of us. "Fine. But I know you'll get the job. And I will nail the audition, I promise. I won't disappoint you. Not as an actor, and not as your fake fiancé," I said confidently. "So we don't really need to worry about money. We're both going to get something we want out of this. I will be your perfect pretend boyfriend."

She smiled. "I knew you were the right man for the job. We'll have dinner at their penthouse Friday night."

"Sounds like a blast," I said, and truth be told, I meant it fully. I didn't hate the idea of seeing Sutton "off-hours," fake boyfriend or not. Out of the office, with no money at stake, there was some wiggle room, so to speak. Room to think about undoing a few more buttons on her shirt and getting a glimpse of what those sexy collarbones hinted at.

She rose, held out her hand for shaking. I looked at it, then at her as I stood. This was another opportunity. "That's not exactly how I'd seal a deal with my fiancée." I moved her hand out of the way and stepped closer. "And I bet that's not how you'd do it, either."

"Do I hear a counteroffer?" She cupped her hand to her ear, cocking her head.

The temptation was too great, and I leaned close enough to tease her with a whisper. "Let's start with a hug."

She shivered and slanted me a doubtful look. "A hug?"

"It's easy," I said, taking her hand and putting it on my shoulder. "You put your hand here, and I'll put mine here . . ." I slid my arm to circle her waist.

"Excuse me, Ms. Brenner . . ." A voice boomed through the speakerphone on Sutton's desk. "There's a Janelle Pinkerton here to see you."

6

SUTTON

I snapped back from Reeve like a teenager caught with a boy in her room. "Bloody hell," I muttered and pressed a hand against my suddenly racing heart. "What could she want?" It felt as though she was checking up on me—a product of my guilty conscience, or perhaps my fear of being found out before the ruse had even started.

Reeve studied my reaction. "This is the woman we need to convince?"

"The very same." I hid a grimace as I walked over to the phone. "Go ahead and send her in please." Then I turned to answer Reeve's unspoken question. "She's on the producing team. So, time to improvise."

"Ah. I see." He stretched an arm across the back of the sofa, settling into character, I supposed. Just moments later, Janelle walked into the office, a thin-lipped smile on her face.

"Hello, Ms. Brenner."

"So good to see you again, Mrs. Pinkerton."

Janelle cast a glance at Reeve on the couch, then back at me with an arched eyebrow. "I didn't mean to interrupt you."

"Actually, the timing is perfect. This is my, er, fiancé."

Janelle seemed to catch my stumble over the unfamiliar word, and her arched brows made me nervous. I suddenly didn't know what to do with my hands, and I had new sympathy for the actors who auditioned for me.

With remarkable aplomb, Reeve stood up, drawing Janelle's attention, and then took her hand and placed a kiss near her wrist. "Such a pleasure to meet you," he said, distractingly roguish.

Even thin-lipped Janelle wasn't immune, it seemed. "And you as well. I had no idea I'd be lucky and meet you so early."

"I can't wait for Friday night," Reeve said. "Can I bring anything? I'm not a very good cook, but I will tell you this—I can bake the best chocolate chip cookies in the world." Then he flashed a smile at Janelle, and I marveled at the ease with which he slid right into his role as fictional fiancé.

"Oh, I do love a good chocolate chip cookie," Janelle said, and I was sure it was the first time I'd seen the woman smile. She turned to me, and I tried not to look wary. "I stopped by since I was in the area. Johnathan and I have extra seats in our box at the theater tomorrow night. I know it's short notice but . . ."

She opened her purse and took out an envelope,

then two tickets out of that. "If you can join us, we'd be *so* pleased."

"Oh. How kind of you to think of me—I mean, us." Would it be suspicious to avoid being around the Pinkertons? On one hand, it *was* last minute. On the other hand, I didn't want to miss any opportunity to distinguish myself from the rest of the list.

Reeve rescued me again, smoothly taking the tickets from Janelle and picking up the conversation. "Sut and I will confer on our schedules, but I have heard great things about this play. I mentioned it the other morning while we were walking The Artful Dodger. And now, look at this. You give us tickets. It's like serendipity." He flashed his utterly disarming smile.

I didn't allow myself a sigh of relief, but I felt it. On the fly, he'd come up with a cutesy nickname— even though I was not a nickname type, it sounded just right from a fiancé—and worked in personal details of my daily routine. In fact, he was so convincing, I found myself wondering what route we'd taken through the park.

"I'm Reeve Larkin, by the way." His easy smile smoothed over my lapse in introductions. "Love your movies. All of them," he said.

"Well, aren't you kind," Janelle said to his acknowledgement of her behind-the-scenes efforts, looking almost human. Then she resettled her designer purse against her side. "Well, I better be on my way. I'm sure you two have plans for the rest of the day." Then she lowered her voice to a whisper and winked. "A little session on the casting couch, perhaps?"

I was shocked and caught my jaw hanging open. It was hard to close when I was stunned and indignant that she'd think I would stoop to casting couch shenanigans—ever, but especially in the wake of the #metoo movement. Even industry people without ethics didn't so much as joke about such things. And I had plenty of ethics—

Or at least I did before I hired an actor as my fake fiancé to get a job. Remembering that robbed the moral high ground as well as any argument.

But almost as shocking was that the wink and innuendo came from *Janelle Pinkerton*, who had seemed so conservative—even prudish—in the meeting just this morning. I'd have thought I'd imagined it if not for Reeve's sheepish shrug.

"What can I say?" He moved over to drape an arm over my shoulder. My skin heated wherever he touched me, and to my surprise, I shivered as he ran his thumb against the fabric of my shirt. "Sometimes I just need to stop by and visit my woman in the middle of the day."

Janelle slyly nodded, as if she understood exactly what Reeve meant when I wasn't even sure myself. I suddenly felt unmoored, as if Reeve and Janelle were in on some secret and I—the one who'd engineered this fake engagement—was the clueless one.

"See you at the theater," Janelle said as she turned and started down the hallway. She glanced back, and with perfect timing, Reeve pressed his lips lightly against mine. I was so off-balance and tense that the kiss surprised me when it shouldn't have, and I jumped.

"Oh!"

I looked down the hall, and thankfully, Janelle was gone, so she wouldn't wonder why I reacted so strangely from a kiss from my fiancé.

"You okay?" Reeve asked.

"Absolutely," I assured him—us both, really. "Just startled is all."

He slid his arm from my shoulders and stepped back, but not much. "Well, if we're going to pull this off, you might want to get used to me kissing you. Just a suggestion."

"Right. I should definitely get used to that." I nodded resolutely. What I really needed to do was get my groove back. I was a take-charge kind of woman and needed to start steering this ship properly. If that meant getting used to kisses, so be it. If that meant reviewing the basics of our relationship so I could say the word fiancé without choking on it, then I'd do that too.

I placed a hand on a hip and appraised Reeve from top to bottom. "I think we're going to need a better outfit for you to go to the theater. We do have box seats."

"What?" Indignantly, he smoothed an invisible tie. "You don't think I have nice clothes for the theater? I didn't just fall off the turnip truck yesterday, you know."

"Hmm. The implication that you fell off the turnip

truck at any point in your history makes me think we need a shopping trip."

He folded his arms. "All right, Professor Higgins. Have it your way."

"I usually do."

I didn't realize how . . . sexual that sounded until Reeve's eyes darkened suddenly and he darkened his voice to match, not quite growling, "If you want to change that up, let me know."

The heat spreading over my face must have been a flush because I was not a woman who blushed at such a subtle innuendo. I looked at my watch and pretended I didn't notice it. I'd have to point out it was inappropriate, since this was a job, and I didn't actually mind.

"I have to make some calls on this TV guest doctor role I'm casting for *Overnight Shift* next Monday," I said, referring to the popular medical drama. I'd written down my list of ten potentials this morning on the cab ride over to my office, pulling them from my mental rolodex. "I need about fifteen minutes. Can you wait in the lobby, and then we'll go to Elizabeth's and get you a new shirt and pants?"

He nodded, and I returned to my office and shut the door. I sank down into my chair and scrolled through my files to find the numbers of the agents I had to call. I could multitask, though, and popped open my text app in one corner of the screen.

Sutton: I might have made a terrible mistake.

McKenna: How terrible? I'm in the middle of something and it's going to be hard to get free to fly to NY and help you bury a body.

Sutton: No one's dead yet.

McKenna: Is the fire department involved?

Sutton: If you mean literal fire, then no.

McKenna: Oh boy! Metaphorical flames? Is it the hot hipster? Did you audition him? And by "audition" I mean that as dirty as it sounds.

Sutton: No! Well. Not really. I had him come into the office, and then Janelle Pinkerton came in and now there's no turning back because she met him and gave me tickets to the theater.

McKenna: The theater. That's some commitment right there.

Sutton: Box seats. And now that I'm thinking about it, that seems a little out of the blue. What if she didn't want to wait until Friday to vet my fiancé?

McKenna: Make sure he's real, you mean?

Sutton: Exactly. And now she wants to see how we act together.

McKenna: I would say that you sound paranoid, except that your fiancé *didn't* exist until this morning. Is Reeve the mistake? Maybe you don't have the chemistry to be convincing?

Sutton: Trust me. Lack of chemistry is not the problem.

McKenna: Ha! I knew it!

Sutton: I can't believe you made me admit that so quickly.

McKenna: Just being efficient. I'm afraid I don't see the problem here. You wanted someone who was your type, right?

Sutton: It's like I ordered him custom-tailored . . . Oh, wait. I did.

McKenna: Isn't that good? Attraction will make you more convincing as a couple, right?

Sutton: That's true.

* * *

I drummed my fingers on the desk as I waited for the voicemail beep on the last agent on my list and thought about McKenna's point. When I cast a play, I was always looking for that indefinable spark between actors. The best in the world could only do so much without chemistry to work with.

And my chemistry with Reeve gave him a lot to work with. I just needed to keep my perspective. I wanted Janelle Pinkerton to believe Reeve was madly in love with me. I didn't want to start believing it myself.

7

SUTTON

On the way to the men's department at Elizabeth's, Reeve and I walked past the jewelry counters. I started to veer that way—I do that, like a squirrel drawn by shiny objects—then stayed on task.

Reeve missed nothing, though. He slowed and gestured to the counter. "Did you want to stop? I'm not in a hurry."

I waved the idea away. "Another time. Nothing is really catching my attention."

"You can tell that from over there?"

"I have a good eye."

"Don't sell yourself short." He gave that lopsided grin. "You have *lovely* eyes."

Perhaps, but I rolled them at that comment. "Let's go use them to find you something to wear."

He made that smile look challenging somehow. "You really do like to have your way, don't you? I might point out that a good relationship is built on compromise." He moved over to let a woman pass pushing a high-end baby stroller. His shoulder brushed mine, and a wave of tingles spread from that point.

That was good. McKenna was right. This attraction would sell our story, which would keep me in the running for the job. I should just think of any time Reeve and I spent together as prep work. Whenever I pitched new producers, I researched the production company, all their films or shows, and any personal details that would help me make a connection. When I could, I found out as much as I could about the project they wanted to cast, the roles, and what type of actors they seemed to prefer.

For this, I needed to make sure we were convincing on a non-verbal level—which was where the chemistry came in—and that we had our backstory straight.

"Right," I said, intending to make the best use of our time shopping. "We can practice compromising while we work on our backstory. I want to make sure all the details are ironclad. I propose we go with the truth as to how we met—I cast you in a day part for *It's Raining Men.*"

"Yes, dear. I remember how we met."

I slanted a glance at him as we walked. Yes, he was joking. I wanted to keep an emotional safety zone, but not to alienate him. Rapport—that's what I was aiming for. "So, let's start with the basics. Janelle already knows your name, since you met her already."

"Damn."

I stopped walking and looked at him in not-quite alarm. "What?"

"I wanted to be a Sven."

That surprised a laugh out of me. "Sven?"

"Don't I look like a Sven? What do you think?" He struck a model pose, tilting his head to highlight his cheekbones and jaw. The fact that he knew exactly how to do that was a good reason to keep telling myself "rapport" until it stuck.

"You don't, actually, look like a Sven. Sorry."

With a huge sigh, he let his shoulders droop. "Okay, I guess."

We continued toward the men's section at a less purposeful clip. "So, I'm Reeve Larkin from Ohio. My dad's a cop. My mom's a teacher. I went to Ohio State."

I rolled my eyes. "Very funny."

"What's wrong with that?"

"No one will buy that. It's such a cliché. Cop dad and teacher mom? You look straight out of Central Casting—the too-good-to-be-true boy from Middle America who went to the hometown college to boot. Did you have a Collie named Shep too? Or was it Rex?"

"Lady, actually." I glanced at him and found humor but no cheekiness. "It's the truth, I swear. Studied American Lit for my major."

"Okay, fine. Best we work with that."

"Good. It's easy to remember, being as it, you know, happened."

I kept my eyes forward, not hiding my smile, but

not ceding the win, either. "And we started dating shortly after the premiere of *It's Raining Men* six months ago."

"Ah, May is the perfect time to begin a love story. And you looked so incredible at the premiere in that slinky black dress."

I stopped walking, putting a hand on Reeve's arm so he stopped too. "You remember the dress I wore?"

He made a *pfft* sound like it was no big deal. "You're gorgeous. You cast me in a movie. Yes, I remember."

Biting my lip, I fought to ignore the feeling that swept through me. It *was* a very big deal, somehow, in some way I'd better examine alone at home.

"So . . ." I continued with our fabled affair, "we went out the next night."

"To Italian," he added. "Because that's my favorite. Along with grapefruit."

I gave him the side-eye. "I don't think I've ever had grapefruit served with Italian food."

"Independently, not concurrently."

"I'm vastly relieved they're not getting up to some kind of culinary abomination fusion food in Ohio."

Reeve rolled his eyes. "Oh, she's a lady boss, a comedienne, and a food critic too." But he smiled crookedly when he looked at me again. "This is where you tell me your favorite food."

"Fish and chips."

He stared for a moment, then shook his head. "You have no business telling me that I am playing to the cliché."

"I like tea too," I said, then I let my folded arms and most British stare serve as the rest of my reply, and from his chuckle, it served well.

"So tell me something I don't know about Sutton Brenner's usual day."

"Get up, walk the dog for an hour . . ."

"Hmm. This might be the time to discuss compromise as I raise the question of how early we have to get up to take the dog for a walk."

"We?"

"I can't walk the dog with you?"

How could a question be as powerful as a kiss or a touch? Something like goose bump shivers shook me as I considered the idea of us walking The Artful Dodger together, mostly moving at our usual power-walk pace, sometimes, maybe on Sunday morning, taking it at a leisurely, couple-time stroll. When had I last had that kind of togetherness with someone?

"If you can keep up with us." I kept it light. "I need to buy him a new jacket, though. Last year's fleece has gotten tatty, and it's getting colder." The poor little love had been shivering this morning, and moving as fast as his little legs could manage. "I also do yoga and Pilates."

"Of course. What's your favorite book? Wait. It has to be *Oliver Twist*. Because of your dog."

I flashed him another grin. "Heavens. Somebody *was* a Lit major in college, after all."

"Well, it's not rocket science, since your dog *is* named after a character in the book. Is your Artful Dodger a pickpocket too?"

"Nope. Trained him out of it. Your favorite book?"

"Toss-up between *Fear and Loathing in Las Vegas* or *The Great Gatsby*."

Those were good picks. He had excellent taste. More points in his favor. "Favorite movie?"

"Anything you've cast," he said with a wink.

I arched a brow playfully. "Oh, we are a perfect pair. That's my favorite movie too."

"Okay, when are we moving in together?"

"After the wedding. I'm old-fashioned."

"Right. Virtue. On the subject of virtue, what's your favorite position?" Reeve asked as we walked past high-heeled shoes.

I stopped. "Excuse me?"

"Well, I'm not buying the protecting-the-virtue thing. I doubt they will either. So, what is it?"

"I highly doubt that will come up at dinner. Besides, our deal was for pretend. So I don't think we need to go there."

"No. We don't need to go there. But yet, that Janelle . . ." He trailed off without finishing the thought.

That drew my attention. Had he sensed something from her? Some suspicion? "What do you mean, *That Janelle?*"

He shrugged as he stroked his chin. "I don't know, but her casting couch comment made me think she's not quite as conservative as she pretends to be."

"And because of that, we need to prepare a briefing doc on our fictional sex life?" I raised an eyebrow, daring him to keep going.

He didn't answer right away. Instead, he swept a strand of my soft brown hair behind my ear and asked in a low, sexy voice, "What could it hurt for me to know how you like it, Sutton?"

Oh, he was good. He was very, very good, because I felt that swooping feeling in my belly. But I wasn't going to be rattled by it. I was going to play along too. I took a step closer to Reeve, giving him a "you naughty boy" look. Wetting my bottom lip, I whispered, "I like it on all fours, from behind, feeling hands on my back and in my hair and gripping my hips." His chest rose and fell, and he pressed his lips together, as if he were trying to hold back a word, or maybe even a moan as I followed up with a question, asking, "What's yours, Reeve?"

He locked eyes with me, and goose bumps spread over my arms. Then, he dipped in closer, his mouth inches away. "That one. The one you like best. That's my favorite. My favorite thing is making you feel good."

I drew in a sharp breath, then clamped my lips closed. But it was too late. A fuse had lit inside me. Deep in my belly, sending heat throughout my body, sending warmth between my legs. Then I reminded myself—he was an actor; he was playing the role I'd cast him in. But oh, he could sweep the awards with the way he'd said *making you feel good*. It seemed so true and authentic, as if Reeve really had made me feel all those things in the bedroom and would again.

"We better get moving." I led him to the men's section, choosing several high-end dress shirts for him, sharp pants, and a few neat ties. Much safer topics.

I held a green button-down against him. "This shirt is perfect for your eyes."

"I feel like Julia Roberts in *Pretty Woman*," he joked.

"Cue the shopping montage," I said. "I do love a good shopping montage. Arms loaded with clothes, rejected outfits flying over dressing room doors . . ."

"May I help you with that?"

The question came from a cute, perky dressing room attendant. Reeve nodded, and the woman took the potential purchases and showed him to a dressing room. I sat on the leather couch just outside and took out my phone, firing off a few quick replies to agents asking questions about next Monday's plastic surgeon audition. Were there pages? Yes, already attached. How should the actors dress? In scrubs. Clean-shaven look or stubble? Stubble, but of course. But I couldn't help picturing Reeve pulling off his T-shirt, standing there alone in the dressing room, shirtless, only jeans on.

Damn. He made it hard to concentrate. I took off my glasses and pressed on the bridge of my nose as if I could push away all the thoughts of him.

The attendant walked by. "If you want to go in and help your boyfriend choose a shirt, it's totally fine with me."

Apparently, Reeve had the same idea, because I heard him call out to me. "Hey, Sut. I could use a little help."

8

REEVE

A boyfriend would definitely want to show potential purchases to his girlfriend, I reasoned. This was part of the role, and I had to play it well. I wanted to impress her. I wanted something else, but I had to think about how to go about it—or rather, if I should.

The thing was, I'd meant to be provoking, asking about her sexual preferences. But oh, had it backfired, when her answer finally came, all smoky and breathy and accompanied by images of trailing a hand down her naked, gorgeous back.

To play this part, I had to ask myself, what would Reeve do if he was dating this beautiful, sexy woman? I'd follow-up on the interest I glimpsed when she was off her guard. I'd test the waters and let her know I was open to any invitation. No strings, no contract, no conditions.

That's what was on my mind as I opened the door a bit and watched her walk toward me. She had a hell of a body, a true hourglass shape. I could picture her on top of me, imagine wrapping my fingers around her waist. Or her pressed against the wall, that fabulously sculpted ass of hers jutting out, and I could hold her that way.

My eyes drank her in as she gave a perfunctory rap of the knuckles on the open door.

"Funny. I thought you had clothes to show me." Sutton slid inside the dressing room. When she pointed to my naked chest, she came within a hair's breadth of touching me, but I felt it as if she had. "Did you need me to help get your shirt on?"

"On. Off. Ladies' choice." I closed the door behind us.

"Doubt the theater has a shirts optional policy. So *on*, don't you think?" she asked, sounding the tiniest bit breathy. She could talk a good game, but her gaze kept drifting to my chest and abs. I worked out a lot. I didn't just need to look good, I needed to look better than any other actor auditioning for the same parts.

"Okay. Let's try this green one." I started to reach for a shirt. She stopped me.

"You have a tattoo." With avid eyes, she pointed to the swirling calligraphy that lined one side of me, from my hip bone up to my arm.

This couldn't be news to her. But maybe she was noticing it in a whole new way. "You've seen my tattoo. You required shirts off for *It's Raining Men.*"

"I know," she started, but her voice was shaky. "I just haven't seen it this close."

And I threw caution to the wind. Here we were in a tiny space, and we were playing our parts. "Want to touch?" I asked, and I really wanted her to say yes.

She did so with a nod, then reached out as if she were mesmerized, as if she were lured in by some uncontrollable force toward my skin, my muscles, my body. She started at the hip bone, one fingertip making contact. She glanced up, and I drew in a breath. In this moment, I wasn't acting. As she trailed a finger up my side, everything about her touch made me buzzed. I wanted to grab her and do everything, but I let myself exist in the moment, in the way she seemed so drawn to the marks I'd made on my body.

"They look like very fancy letters. Three of the letter H?"

"They are. For the three most important things in the world," I answered.

"And those are?"

"Health. Happiness. And hope."

She gave me a quick smile. "Yes. I agree." Then she traced her fingertip from my chest down to my waist as if she were painting my skin. Her touch was as soft as a butterfly, but it was full of fire, and I liked it. Her fiancé would know if and how she liked to be touched too.

"This is more convincing now."

She tilted her head as if to ask what I meant. "I'm not sure I'm following?"

"You were all weird and awkward when I kissed you at your office," I added, pointing out the truth.

"I'm sorry. I was just surprised."

"I know. But don't jump the next time I kiss you. We need to work on that."

"We do?"

"Well, that would give it away, wouldn't it? You need to get used to being kissed by me."

"Okay," she said with a businesslike nod.

"That means we need to practice."

"Practice kiss," she said slowly, then nodded quickly. "Right. Of course. Like actors. Like a stage kiss."

She sounded chipper and cheery, as if she were trying to convince herself. Whatever worked for her, I'd go along with it. "Think of this as a dress rehearsal. We're prepping for the big kiss scene that makes the audience swoon and totally believe we're in love. Got it?"

She nodded.

"Ready?"

"Right here in the dressing room?"

"What better place to dress-rehearse a kiss than a dressing room?"

"Totally. Absolutely. Definitely."

I wondered how many more adverbs she'd need either to work up to a kiss that was meant to be seen instead of private, or to get over whatever her hesitation might be. She was terrifically sexy and sensual, but it was intimidating knowing your kiss would be analyzed and critiqued. I'd have to take the lead.

So I looked at her, as if she were the woman I'd

been dying to kiss for years. She was my leading lady, the only woman I wanted. She returned my gaze, and then it was as if a flame burst. I pictured her ravenous and greedy, wanting to be consumed with kisses. Her lips were parted slightly, and her breathing had become . . . lustful. Maybe she was acting too. In that moment, I didn't care. I wanted to taste her lips, to feel more of her beautiful body. There was something about her, maybe it was the age difference, her twenty-eight to my twenty-four, or maybe it was the power play. But there was no time for analysis because my head was turning cloudy with a need I hadn't had before. I wanted to do things to this woman. I wanted to make her feel the way a good boyfriend would—desired, wanted, craved. She deserved all that. I could give it to her now. I could give it to her for a week.

"You look like you want something," I whispered.

She didn't answer. She just licked her lips once. That was enough of an answer. That was all I needed. I moved behind her, brushed a strand of hair away from her neck, and pressed my naked chest against her back. I watched her in the mirror as she closed her eyes and sighed into me.

I started with her neck, pressing my lips gently against her skin. She smelled like some kind of shampoo, jasmine maybe, and she moaned the moment I touched her. It was like a chemical reaction, the two of us. We had that kind of physical attraction that smacks you hard and turns you inside out in a second.

Instant and electric, and you feel like you can set the
world on fire. We could have known each other for
years or been two strangers who met on a train—our
bodies were magnets for each other. With the softest
of flutters, I kissed her neck, barely touching her, but
touching her enough to make her move, to make her
shift her hips against me. Running my hands down
her back, I rested my palms on her waist, and she
gasped. I worked my way to her ear, nibbling the
earlobe, then kissing her jawline as she said my name
in a low voice that gave all her desires away. "Reeve."

Her voice was needy, full of want. I turned her
around, zeroed in on her red lips, then gave her a soft,
silver-screen kiss. Not the kind that leads to the
bedroom. But the kind you give at the front door at
the end of a fantastic date. Tender, gentle, lingering.

She was such an alpha woman in the workplace—all
take-charge and full-speed-ahead. But here, in my
arms, she was different. She seemed vulnerable, like she
was letting down her guard. She was the sexy librarian
unpinning her hair and taking off her glasses for me.

She kissed back just as gently. A sweet slide.

The kiss lasted all of five seconds. Maybe ten.

It could have lasted all day and I wouldn't want to
end it.

"How is it going in there?" The voice of the attendant cut in. "Are you finding anything to your liking?"

And I broke the kiss. Sutton's eyes were glossy, her
expression kiss-drunk. Hell, that was a good look
for her.

It probably matched mine.

I needed to collect myself, though. I cleared my throat, keeping my eyes on the woman in front of me as I answered, "Yes. Everything is to my liking."

The attendant walked away, and Sutton and I stood, awkward and—in my case, at least—feeling foolish, as if we'd been caught red-handed doing something childish instead of oh-so-adult.

"So," I said, drawing the word out as she brushed her hands against her skirt, looking everywhere but at me. "I guess that might seem a bit more believable if we have to kiss in front of anyone."

"Yes. I think that might convince people."

I reached for her chin, softly raising her face so she had to meet my eyes. "See. Rehearsals are fun."

"Indeed," she said, and shot me a smile that I recognized. I'd seen her give it to every actor after their audition—her "next item of business" smile.

Fine, we needed to get back on task.

"I suppose I should figure out what I'm going to wear tomorrow," I said. Maybe the attendant's visit was the reminder I needed too—this was a job, and I shouldn't fuck it up by feeling too much.

Sutton shifted gears, back to being the sassy, in-control businesswoman. "Okay, darling. Let's get you in some clothes. Any pretend boyfriend of mine better look absolutely fetching for the theater."

I nodded and slid into a crisp button-down, modeling the shirt for Sutton. She curled up her lips, narrowed her eyes, and nodded approvingly. I tried on a few more, and she ticked each one off as a yes too.

"Lucky me. Who knew I was going to come away with a dashing, debonair wardrobe as part of this gig?"

"Isn't that one of the great benefits of being an actor? You often get to take home the costumes."

The bell rang over the door of the bakery as I perused the display cases full of cakes, pastries, and other delicious treats. I needed a gift for an agent who'd called in a favor recently on my behalf. My thoughts wandered to Reeve idly imagining what he might like and what, if we were truly together, I might pick up and bring home to my fiancé as a little, "just because" surprise.

I caught myself and stomped on the brakes before I could go farther down that road. As delicious as our kiss was—and it was divine—we weren't a "just because" gift couple. We weren't a couple at all. We had a business deal. The end.

On the counter, I spotted a Swedish Fish lying atop what looked like a Rice Krispy treat. The sign read *Today's Special: Candy Sushi.*

"Tell me, Josie," I said, looking up to meet the green-eyed gaze of the shop owner, a woman I had grown friendly with recently since Sunshine Bakery had become my top source when I wanted to thank a colleague, contact, or friend, or just didn't want to show up empty-handed. "Candy sushi . . . Is that as decadent as it sounds?"

Josie smiled brightly as she tucked a strand of pink-tipped brown hair behind her ear. "Decadent, delicious, and divine."

A male voice chimed in. "Don't undersell it, Josie. Tell her the truth. They're orgasmic."

I turned toward the man, and oh my . . . He was quite a specimen. Tall, dark hair, hazel eyes, chiseled jaw. What a shame I had just cast *Overnight Shift*, or I'd hire him immediately to play a sexy doctor. But judging from the scrubs he wore, he might already play that role in real life.

"Orgasmic, you say? That's quite an endorsement," I said. The conversation at least steered my mind away from the man I shouldn't, couldn't be buying a treat for.

Sexy Doctor tapped his chest. "I speak the truth when it comes to Josie's treats."

"He taste-tested them for me before I added them to the specials list," Josie said, then she called out to the handsome doctor. "Thanks for saying orgasmic in front of my customer, Chase."

I laughed. Josie knew I wouldn't be bothered in the least by that word.

He pretended to be aghast. "So sorry for my dirty mouth."

His gaze stayed on the pretty baker, and I made a mental note to ask Josie the next time I came to the shop what was up with her and the sexy man in the scrubs. There was some kind of energy working between the two of them, clear as day as he chatted with us while Josie boxed up the treats. Did Reeve and I have that kind of energy?

Well, for show, of course. That's the only reason I was wondering as much.

As I said goodbye and went to drop off the gift, I turned my brain away from other potential lovers and onto my very own date tonight.

I applied mascara, the finishing touch for tonight. I'd always believed that it was the vitamin of makeup, the most essential one, and one should never leave the house without it.

"Right, my lovely Artful Dodger. You agree, don't you?"

I stroked my Chihuahua/Min Pin between the ears, and he looked up at me lovingly with those big wet eyes that always melted me. "Oh, you are my sweet, aren't you?"

The Artful Dodger was sitting on the vanity in my bathroom, as he often did. He had bathroom counter privileges, but only when I was applying makeup. I put the mascara wand away, brushed one hand against the other, and declared, "That's that."

Then I scooped up my nine-pound fur baby, brought him to my bedroom and deposited him gently on the burnished gold comforter.

I stepped back and held out my arms. "What do you think, sweetheart? I'm going for dramatic but not theatrical. Even though I will be acting the part of a fiancée." The slinky gray dress hugged my hips, and I wore it with knee-high black boots and a silky red wrap thrown over my shoulders. The Artful Dodger yawned, turned in a circle twice, and curled up in a furry donut on the comforter.

"I'm not going to take the yawn as editorial," I told him. "I'm nervy enough as it is. My look is at least one thing I don't have to worry about."

I had the tickets in a small clutch purse, and as I grabbed the purse from the bed and took one last look in the mirror, I thought about the dressing room yesterday. Reeve kissed like he'd been custom-made for kissing me. I'd always wanted to be drowned in kisses, and his lips traveling over my neck, raising gooseflesh, making my insides quiver . . . I wanted him, and that was no act.

He'd seemed to want me too. He seemed to radiate hunger for me. But that's why I'd hired him—to *seem* to want me. I'd enlisted him to play a part, and he was playing it so well, it was easy to buy into the performance—to never question that the kiss was legit.

Even when I questioned it, there was a tiny voice that pointed out, why should he pretend with no audience?

I sighed, adjusted my wrap, and bent down to kiss my dog on his soft brown fur. "At least I know you'll always be here for me, my love."

I needn't worry about messy things like a bloom of

feelings for a pretend boyfriend. The Artful Dodger licked my hand once and curled into a tighter dog-ball.

Reeve and I had arrived at the theater minutes apart from each other. We went in together, easily finding the box. The Pinkertons were already there, Janelle with her hair slicked back in that tight-as-a-ballerina-bun and Johnathan looked admittedly nice in a custom suit. He rose and greeted me warmly. There was nothing unprofessional about it, but I was aware, even if he wasn't, of Janelle watching for him to put a toe out of line.

Though, from the frown he gave her as he stepped back, he read her perfectly well.

"How lovely that you could join us," Janelle said, giving me air kisses on each cheek. Maybe she transformed after dark, because she seemed almost human. "And what a pleasure to see Mr. Larkin again. Reeve, please meet my husband."

Reeve shook hands with Johnathan, and they exchanged hellos. If Reeve was nervous to meet a producer with the power to make or break an actor's career, he gave no sign of nerves. In fact, he segued quickly into discussing golf, at first surprising me, because I never would have taken him for a golfer, and then impressing me, because I realized he'd done his research too. He was truly convincing as he conversed with Johnathan on the best type of golf swing.

"Looks like they're old chums," I said to Janelle with a smile.

She gave a put-upon sigh. "Are you destined to be a golf-widow as well, or is Reeve just a quick study?"

I was prepared for any question about our relationship, but not about golf. Whatever my face did, it made Janelle smirk, and my heart sank. "Please," she said. "You pretended admirably, but I can tell Reeve is the actor—I actually can't tell if he likes golf or not."

"I . . . uh . . ." I had no words. No words that weren't full of panic. If I gave the game away on such a minor detail, how was I going to maintain the fiction of the fiancé?

Another sigh from Janelle as a pretty usher with a perky figure walked by and Johnathan's eyes followed her. "There are worse things than golf he could be doing. Something to keep in mind."

I remained speechless.

But she was taking care of business.

"Johnathan," she said sharply, sounding exactly like I did when I called The Artful Dodger to heel when he was misbehaving (which was never). So sharply that all three of us jumped.

Conversation about golf and anything else stopped, and Johnathan looked like—well, he looked like The Artful Dodger when called out for misbehaving. Reeve and I floundered at the edge on this awkward conversational sinkhole that just opened up in front of us while the Pinkerton couple had another one of their subtextual conversations.

Flummoxed, Reeve looked at me, and I shrugged helplessly.

Quick, quick, think of something, anything, *to fill the dead air.* The weather? The Pinkertons had a Siamese cat named Archibald. Perhaps, I should chat about pets? Pets? Who didn't like to talk about their pets?

But Reeve spoke, asking if they'd seen an Oscar winner performing in a play at the Eugene O'Neill theater last week. "He was as amazing as the critics say," Reeve added.

Janelle relinquished her sharp-eyed stare and turned to Reeve. "Frankly, I don't often care for big movie stars in Broadway plays. But he is the exception. A rare breed who can handle theater and film."

Reeve nodded thoughtfully. "I hear you. It can be a little distracting with movie stars, but then, he's one of a kind. What about you, Mr. Pinkerton? What else have you been to?"

They all chatted for a few minutes about the theater, and I was relieved that Johnathan's wayward glance hadn't unraveled the night completely.

"And what do you do, Reeve? Forgive me for not asking when we first met yesterday," Janelle said.

"I'm an actor," he said, with a touch of pride.

"How marvelous," Mr. Pinkerton chimed in. "And how did you two meet?"

It was a natural question, and we'd prepared for it, but I still felt like a jangly mess of nerves. Was Janelle onto us? Was that why she was here? To check the details of the engagement for consistency?

"On the job," Reeve answered. "Sut cast me in *It's Raining Men*, and the day of the premiere, I asked her out. I couldn't resist. She was smart, and she was beautiful, and that was all it took. I've only had eyes for her since then."

Reeve looked at me, his brown eyes were so warm and true—they seemed to speak all the things he was saying, as if his words came genuinely from his heart.

"And the wedding is when?"

There was a lag while Janelle's question went from my ear to my brain and went roundabout once or twice until memory tapped me on the shoulder and said she was talking to me. Even then, I just blinked, my mouth going dry as Janelle frowned at me. My boardroom confidence had packed its bags and gone on holiday. But I couldn't help feeling that Janelle knew I lied and was trying to catch me. Maybe I wouldn't feel so at sea if I could better read the woman. Or read her at all—one minute the woman was generous and warm, the next she was the ice queen. If she'd just settle on one or the other, I didn't entirely care which it was.

Once again, Reeve threw me a lifeline. Clasping my hand tightly in his, he told Janelle, "May. One year after our first date. I was ready to elope, but Sut insisted we have a real wedding, and we were lucky enough to reserve the sculpture garden at MoMA. A late Sunday afternoon was all they had, but we weren't going to let that opportunity pass. It was one of our first dates."

Janelle immediately seemed to soften. Maybe she simply liked Reeve better than she liked me. Sexism emerged in the oddest ways. That Janelle was another of our outnumbered gender in the industry didn't preclude her from freezing out the woman—which was to say the descendant of Eve and tempter of husbands—and warming to a gorgeous young man.

Not only because of his looks. Reeve was unnervingly adept at playing this woman. Perhaps all women. I hated that thought even though I benefited now from the way he spun a tale and soon had the tightly wound producer's wife eating out of his palm. Soon, she was chattering about MoMA and her favorite artists, and Reeve was telling her how we flirted in front of an Edward Hopper painting, and Johnathan was looking only at his wife, and Janelle was beaming, and I felt like I could breathe again.

This man—this young, delicious man—was saving the day. I looked up at Reeve, he was easily a good six inches taller, and I felt a rush of affection for him, a surge of gratitude. Impulsively, I stretched to give him a quick kiss on the cheek. He looked at me and shot a quick smile. I might have even seen him blush.

He gestured to the seats, letting the ladies sit first. He sat between us, with Johnathan by Janelle's side. Then I felt Reeve's warm hand and glanced down to see him loop his long, strong fingers through mine and squeeze. It was tender and comforting, and it was exactly what I needed. I leaned into him, resting my head on his shoulder. That was odd. I was never the cuddly type, except when it came to my darling dog.

Soon, the lights dimmed, the curtain rose, and the play began. I sat up straight and focused on the stage, but Reeve kept his fingers linked through mine. As the characters argued about who'd forgotten to do the laundry on time, Reeve began stroking the inside of my palm with his thumb. Light, fluid lines. From my wrist to the edge of my fingers.

It was soft, and it was sweet, and most of all, it was caring. I closed my eyes, giving in to the way his touch felt. It was a caress, a promise. He drew soft little zigzags across my palm, lazy lines that told stories of the two of us, of the things we'd done, the times we'd had, the love we'd shared. Or so it felt as he crept casually past my barriers, his touch making me believe in the fiction of us. Soon, his fingers were tracing the inside of my wrist, then the soft skin on my arm, and then, as all the words spoken from on stage became a distant faraway sound to me, he moved closer, planting a tender, soft kiss on my jawline.

10

REEVE

As I pressed my lips to Sutton's, I couldn't help but notice Janelle sneaking peeks at us, all while her husband focused on the stage like his life depended on it. Why was she watching us now? To appraise the relationship, or for some other reason? Well, I'd been hired for a mission, and I was going to do whatever it took to remove any doubt that Sutton and I were together.

Of course, I didn't mind kissing Sutton. I didn't mind touching her.

Those were both criminal understatements. I relished kissing Sutton, and I loved the way she responded.

Janelle distracted me again by leaning over to her husband and murmuring his name. He snapped his gaze toward her with a different kind of guilt than before—the "I wasn't doing anything this time" look. Closely related to the "What now?" look.

His wife tipped her head toward the exit from the

box. He glared his refusal, and she side-eyed a threat. It was almost more engrossing than the play.

Well, no sense in being polite. It was much more interesting than the play. When Sutton told me that her contract could ride on something like whether she had a fiancé or not, I thought she was exaggerating. I'd heard the gossip about the Pinkertons too, but theater people were dramatic by definition. But holy crap.

It said something about their success as producers that people still wanted to work with them.

Johnathan sneezed, then coughed, then cleared his throat in rapid succession. As someone who'd been trained to do those three things on cue—sometimes, an actor had to sneeze, cough, or clear his throat—I could tell Johnathan was faking it. The man rose, muttered an embarrassed "excuse me," and exited the box.

Janelle grabbed her purse and leaned over to whisper, "Please excuse us, won't you? We'll see you Friday night." With a smile I didn't quite know how to interpret, she added, "There's nothing like watching from the privacy of your own box. So *do* enjoy the rest of the play, you two."

Then she was gone.

Sutton and I stared at their empty seats. "What was that about? They both left?" she asked in a low voice.

"Maybe they didn't care for the play?"

Those two were dysfunctional with a capital D. Tonight's show was a triple feature—the play on stage, the fake fiancé act Sutton and I were putting on, and whatever drama had been happening with the Pinkertons.

I had a part in only one of these, and it deserved my attention. So I layered another kiss below Sutton's earlobe, hearing the breathiest little whisper escape her throat. There was nothing fake about that sound, and I forgot about the Pinkertons and their strange habits, as I found myself drawn back to Sutton's neck, brushing her with another kiss.

Sutton looked at the stage, as if she were enrapt in the acting, and I could have gone back to watching the play. But I'd lost track of whatever the characters were up in arms about, and I didn't really care in the first place. I was much more interested in this woman beside me, in the way she seemed to respond to my touch. I hadn't expected it, but I sure as hell liked the way she seemed to want my hands on her, from the kiss in the dressing room, to now in the theater.

As far as I could tell, there was no reason for me to stop touching Sutton. We were both having a good time, and there was nothing wrong with that.

I brushed a long strand of her hair behind her ear. She shivered, and I loved the way the littlest thing elicited a reaction from her. I bet she'd be a tiger in bed, clawing and moaning, and screaming my name. Damn, I was even more aroused now, picturing the way she must make love, with a sort of fearless abandon. "Do you like the play?"

She swallowed and nodded once. "Very much so."

I glanced back at the entrance to the box seats. The

Pinkertons seemed long gone, there weren't any other ushers nearby, and the closest patrons were in the next box over, a low wall between us. So I went for it. I placed one hand on her opposite cheek and shifted her face toward me, then moved my other hand to her thigh. She looked at me, and even in the dark of the theater, I could read those blue eyes, I could tell they were trying so hard to resist, but yet not wanting to resist in the least. Hell, I didn't either. I moved my thumb along her cheek, tracing a line to her mouth then over her lower lip, when she nipped playfully at the pad of my thumb. I smiled in the dark as I outlined her mouth, then moved down to her neck, memorizing the feel of her throat, the heat from her skin, the way her body seemed to pulse toward me with every touch. Every subtle motion said, "kiss me," and so I took the liberty to do just that.

It was the barest of kisses, the kind that comes at the beginning of something.

As I savored the cherry taste of her mouth, I played with the top of her stockings, slipping a finger along the band that held them in place. Sutton seemed to like me there. She opened her legs the smallest amount, an invitation to explore. I splayed my hand across the top of her thigh, being careful to make sure her dress covered my hand. She bit down on her lip as I inched higher. Another cue. Another sign. I moved closer, sliding my fingers to her panties and pressing against her. There. Between her legs. Where she was already damp beyond words. You couldn't fake that kind of arousal.

And I saw no need to fake my desire. I needed to touch her. Needed it now.

"Can I touch you?" I whispered.

"Please do," she said, and I knew she was aching too, burning with the need to be touched, to feel some kind of release. I slipped my hand into her panties, and she groaned under her breath, leaning her head back. As I stroked her, I imagined her spread out across the chair, arms thrown back, neck long and inviting, legs wide open as I tasted her. God, I wanted to bury my mouth between her thighs, to smell her, inhale her, run a tongue across all that wetness. I wanted to breathe her in and kiss her deeply. She was a feast of a woman; the slightest touch seemed to turn her on, as if she was ready to go at any moment, a live wire, just needing the combustion to set her off.

"I want my tongue between your legs right now," I whispered in a low and husky voice that belied my own reckless thirst for her.

"I want that too," she managed to say as I stroked her, my fingers moving up and down all that glorious wetness. She was trying so hard to be still, to be quiet, as she moved her hips in the smallest of ways, not enough for others to see, but enough for me to know how much she wanted me. I pressed a palm against her, and she let a little moan escape. Then she clasped her hand over her mouth to muffle her noises as I worked her. She was so soft and silky wet; her little breaths were coming faster. She spread her legs another inch or so, and damn, this woman was all fire and heat. I was going to make her come in a

Broadway theater, and I knew in this instant that she was so deep in the throes of passion that she didn't care anymore if anyone saw or anyone heard. She was so far into the crest of the orgasm I was about to give her. I wanted to slam into her, to enter her and feel that wetness wrap around me. But for now, I was thrilled to feel her arch against my hand, once, twice, three times. She inhaled sharply and took several quick deep breaths as she came in my hand.

Gently, carefully, I moved her hand from her mouth and kissed her, just as softly and just as tenderly as I had when I started. Then the curtain fell, and it was time for intermission.

11

SUTTON

Who was this wild woman inhabiting me?

I didn't know who she was.

She seemed to take over when Reeve was around.

And I didn't know what to do with her, so when the play ended we made our way out of the theater onto Eighth Avenue, making small talk about books and such. I looked at the time on my phone and put on a show of remembering how very much I had to do tomorrow.

"Oh my. I nearly forgot about my morning meeting with LGO studios. I must go." I leaned in to give him a kiss on the cheek—for appearances, and all —then I hailed the nearest cab.

"That was the cat's pajamas," I said, slapping on my best smile.

He stared at me as if I didn't quite make sense.

I knew the feeling.

"Pajamas and meow," he said, eyes narrowed.

The cab pulled up and I grabbed the door first,

which surprised him. I gestured for him to get in, even as I realized I couldn't ride anywhere with him. I'd combust. I'd break down. I'd do a hundred unprofessional things.

But I was professional, and I was in control. I needed to remember that.

I needed to remind myself of it just then. I closed the door when Reeve was in the cab and pretended I didn't see his face or hear his "What the hell?" Then I gave the driver cash for the fare to take my date home.

I thought I'd feel better once outside the influence of his vibrant and sexy personality. Less confused and embarrassed. Only now I was just as confused and embarrassed, but lonely too.

I lay wide awake in bed, ashamed. It wasn't something I felt very often.

I stared at the red numbers—3:01 a.m.—reflected on my ceiling from my digital clock. The Artful Dodger was burrowed deep under the covers, curled up at my feet where he slept every night, as I berated myself quietly.

Why had I let things go so far? How out-of-control stupid was I to let Reeve get me off in the theater? My God, I was a businesswoman. I might be known for my taste in man candy, and most of the time I took the winks and nudges in stride. But at the core, it was still my professional area of expertise. That was my eye for talent. Not about some sex-crazed insatiable need to be touched at the cost of my dignity.

I flipped onto my stomach, embarrassed at the thoughts. I loved sex, and I loved men, but I also cherished control. I was much more apt to make the first move, to be the first one to unzip the guy's pants, to take him in my mouth, to bring him to orgasm, than the other way around.

I loved the smell of a man, I loved stubble, I loved that they have stubble, that they can grow it and that they can shave it, I loved how kissing a man was a perfect mix of soft and hard, I loved the smell of soap on a guy's neck, the cut of a firm belly, the feeling of strong arms. But I also loved taking charge, setting the mood, being the first to go below the belt.

Because once I let someone touch me and bring me to that rapturous place of blissful release, I was hooked. I fell quickly, and Reeve was so very fall-for-able. He tied me in knots. He was beautiful, with those soulful eyes that looked as if they'd seen the world even though he was only twenty-four and had probably only seen New York City and Ohio. And his hands . . . He touched me as if I'd given him the secret code to my body, the right numbers and the proper combination, and he'd unlocked me.

But there was more. I felt my heart lunge toward him when he'd saved me back in my office, and then again in the theater with his easy chatter and confident charm. Before he'd even touched my arm, or kissed my jaw, or slid a hand inside my knickers. He'd stepped in and handled the Pinkertons. He'd said the right things, and he'd said them with ease, as if we truly were boyfriend-girlfriend. That was the problem. The way we handled things together—managing the Pinkertons, surviving the painful awkwardness of their company—made me think of us as a team, which was very close to a partnership, which very nearly had me starting to believe the fake relationship that I'd engineered.

I could see myself with him—dating him, going out to dinner and a movie. We would play casting director-in-hindsight, offering opinions on who would really have been best for each part in each flick we saw. Other times, we'd walk my dog in the evenings, picking up a bottle of wine on the way home, enjoying it on my couch as we talked and touched each other all night long, waking up together in the morning.

But that wasn't our reality.

Why had he kept touching me then, after Janelle left? Why perform when no one was watching? I noodled on possibilities until one emerged. He was probably a method actor, immersing himself in the part and staying in the role even when off-stage. I was acting too; I was totally in character.

Besides, I could never fall for an actor, method or not. I worked with them all the time and knew them too well. Even actors and other creative types that I got along with really well, I couldn't imagine dating them. Having a relationship. Never being quite sure what was real emotion, and what was merely an echo of something else.

* * *

Later that day, I swung by Sunshine Bakery to pick up an order of strawberry shortcake cupcakes I planned to take to a studio head.

After Josie finished with her other customers, she grabbed the box of treats and set it in front of me. "These cupcakes will make anyone happy."

I flashed a brief smile, but it didn't feel heartfelt. Josie saw through it right away. "What's wrong? You don't seem yourself."

I shook my head, trying to forget the night before. But that was an impossible pursuit. Besides, sometimes you needed to open up to a friend, and Josie had become one. "Oh you know. I wouldn't admit this to most people, but sometimes I find men terribly vexing."

Josie tossed her head back and cracked up. "Join the club. I'm in the same boat. There's a guy who's driving me crazy right now."

My smile lifted to a more real one now. I did enjoy the chance to hear about other people's lives and loves. "Is there? Do tell. Is it the man in the scrubs?"

Josie's pointed "you guessed it" finger cut my way. "Yeah. He's sexy, smart, funny. Basically, he's everything I could want."

"The full package?"

Josie nodded. "That's a good way to put it."

"And? What's the issue?" I asked. This was good. Focusing on someone else would get my mind off

Reeve. Besides, Josie was a friend and perhaps I could lend an ear.

Josie shrugged. "Just trying to figure out if he wants the same thing from me."

I hummed, fiddling with the box of cupcakes. "Wouldn't it be something if we could order our significant other off of a menu and know exactly what we were getting and what to expect."

"That's the customer service quandary, isn't it," Josie asked, "knowing what a person really wants?"

"As opposed to what they asked for." I nodded sagely. I encountered that often. It was hard to give directors what they wanted in a cast when they didn't really know themselves.

12

REEVE

Bench pressing two hundred fifty pounds was easier than figuring out women. A particular woman, who I mulled over while I worked out at the gym the next morning. My muscles strained, but weight day wasn't quite mentally challenging enough to keep me focused on the here and now instead of last night.

After the play, she was her sassy, playful self, but not once did she mention or even hint at what went down in the box seats. Not that I wanted a blue ribbon or a gold star. But some whisper acknowledging that I'd turned her inside out would have been nice.

I pushed up the barbell, grunting—a little bit from the weight and a lot from the frustration.

One more rep then I lowered the weight, set it down, and headed to the machines, settling in to work on my pecs, moving by rote while my mind circled around again to Sutton.

The lady wanted to act as if nothing had

happened, and I followed her lead, mostly because I didn't have any better idea. What was I going to say —*hey, are we going to talk about how I rocked your world or what?*

Instead, we'd chatted about the play as we left the theater and walked away from the crowds all clumped up to grab taxis. Then we talked about other plays, then books. She quizzed me on why I liked *Fear and Loathing in Las Vegas* until I ran out of answers and felt flustered and put on the spot, like in high school when you dream you're taking an English test on a book you haven't read. Only in that nightmare, I was usually in my underwear. I wasn't opposed to that, but if Sutton wanted to play "Hot for Teacher," she'd been sending the wrong messages. Because I'd simply felt as if I were being grilled, and I didn't know why.

I'd lost track of the reps I'd done on the pectoral machine. Since last night, I'd flipped between confused, pissed, and frustrated then back to confused, like scrolling through 300 satellite channels and starting over.

When we were far enough from the front of the marquee to see an empty cab, she'd hailed one, and when it pulled up to us, she got to the door first and opened it . . . for me. She'd caught me off-balance again, and before I knew it, she'd kissed my cheek and I was in the cab and Sutton was not. While I sorted out what I should or could do about this, she leaned in the driver's window, handed the dude a twenty like I couldn't pay for my own damned taxi, and waved a too-cheery goodbye.

What the hell was that?

She was treating me like a guy treats a girl he doesn't want to see again. *Thanks, babe, here's a cab. I'd say I'll call you, but we know I won't.*

I didn't like it last night, and I was still irritated in the morning. I didn't want the brush-off. I wanted to be seen again, called again, texted again. I wanted a second date with her, dammit.

I finished my reps, breathing hard, trying to shake off these thoughts. What the hell? This was a job, not a real date. It didn't matter who would text the other first, or who said goodbye first or put the other in a cab.

But none of that sensible lecture, not even with her hot-and-cold routine, kept me from wanting her again.

And again.

And maybe one more time.

Yes, I'd like to do bedroom reps with Sutton Brenner.

13

SUTTON

That afternoon, I wrapped up my latest round of calls to agents, requesting callbacks for a part in a TV show. Thanks to my reputation, a premium cable network had contracted me for one of its racier shows about a cadre of Los Angeles party girls who travel to New York City for a bachelorette weekend. The girls go to an invite-only strip club—as one does —for its "Parade of Firemen" night. My task was to find five smoking hot actors who could be the best "firemen" in New York City.

I'd known immediately which of my favorites I wanted to see, but I always liked to give new blood a chance too. Last week I'd spent an afternoon flipping through photos, watching demo reels, and calling the top agents for their input on a few rising stars to mix in. The result had been a visual fiesta at the audition, and though the whole crew had been top-notch, I'd picked the best of the bunch for a callback.

The agents I called today for second looks squeed

and oohed and ahhed, and this was one of my favorite parts of the job—delivering good news. I could either be Santa bringing coal, or Santa bringing gifts, and I'd much rather get to be a Santa who brings a bulging bag of opportunity to hungry actors.

"Great. So the producers will look forward to seeing Joe tomorrow afternoon," I said brightly to Erin, an agent I knew well.

"And Joe will look forward to seeing the producers again," Erin replied. "Also, thanks for the candy sushi. I thought about sharing it with some of my colleagues, but as soon as I finished thinking that, it was all in my belly."

I laughed. "For next week's special, the shop owner is offering grapefruit macarons. I'm pretty sure if anyone can make a grapefruit sing, it's this baker."

"Interesting. That flavor profile would be unexpected. But so would a singing grapefruit," Erin said, and I could hear the wink in her voice.

We wrapped up our conversation, and as I hung up the phone, my mind drifted briefly to grapefruit. Reeve's favorite food. Such an unusual choice, but yet one he seemed committed to. Never met a grapefruit he didn't like, he said. I amused myself imagining how I could put his love to the test—a grapefruit pizza, a grapefruit sandwich, a grapefruit wedge on a bottle of beer.

I caught myself chuckling, and it occurred to me that even the simplest, silliest thoughts of Reeve made my heart dance.

My focus needed to be on work, not grapefruits

and a gorgeous man and whether or not he might like the citrus in a macaron.

I was about to call one more agent when my cell rang. My first thought was that it might be Reeve. But he had no reason to call me before Friday afternoon. And why did I feel like a cocktail of nerves and hope at the possibility it might be my fake fiancé?

But the number was private.

"Sutton Brenner here."

"Good afternoon, Sutton. This is Janelle."

The hopes flew away. The nerves took deeper root. I sat up straight in my chair. "Good afternoon, Janelle. How are you?"

"Did you enjoy the play?"

"Yes. It was fabulous. The seats were amazing. Thank you so much. I hope everything is okay—I know you had to leave early."

"Oh, I saw what I came to see."

I looked at the phone like it might interpret that note in her voice—smug sounding humor of a private joke mixed in with satisfaction. It made her tone sound oddly illicit. Or maybe it was what Reeve had said about her, implying there might be a wild side to Janelle hidden deep—really deep—inside.

It was stressful, not knowing which Janelle I would be dealing with on any day—scary, stern, or salacious. But my stomach was a hard knot as I admitted what I was really afraid of—had she seen what Reeve and I had been up to? Would she call me out on my lack of professionalism?

"In any case, I was calling about something else." If

it were someone besides Janelle Pinkerton, I would have relaxed a little when she changed the subject. "We are so close to making a decision on this film, and one of the things we've yet to determine is the best location in the library to use for the—well, you know."

Right. The library scene. I knew the library scene well. Hell, the world knew the library scene. Flip through any copy of the book and it fell open to that scene from the extra wear, much like the elevator scene in another famous book. In *Escorted Lives*, the woman who falls for her escort takes him to the New York Public Library to show him a rare old book that she wishes she could have for her collection. While at the library, they find a quiet nook and he makes love to her in the stacks.

"Oh. It's been difficult?" I asked, trying to put together the reason she'd called.

Normally, casting directors don't have a role in scouting locations. Our responsibility is to recruit on-camera talent, and the job ends there. It was odd for Janelle to bring up location work with a casting director.

Janelle sighed heavily, as if this issue had been weighing on her. "It is. I went to the library myself, but I can't find a place that's just right. And you have such a good eye for talent that I thought you might have an eye for this as well."

"Okay," I said carefully. I felt as if I were being tested in a new way. There still no ink on this hypothetical deal, but the Pinkertons were asking me to jump through yet another hoop. But I really wanted this job, and having already gotten myself fake-engaged, what was a scouting trip? "Do you want me to go with you?"

"My schedule just won't allow it—another reason I'm calling you, to see if you'd be able to go today. There's a section on Renaissance Astrology on the fourth floor we're thinking about. If you could visualize how the actors would look in that setting and give your opinion, it would help immensely as we get closer to making a decision."

I sighed, keeping it quiet enough that she wouldn't hear. "What is it I should be looking for?"

"I think that section will be a wonderful backdrop for the scene, but Johnathan and the director are quibbling about whether it's the right scale to frame the two actors. And of course, there's the logistics of fitting two people and camera equipment into a private nook. If you could take your fiancé . . . Having Reeve help you would allow you to get a sense of scale. What do you think?"

I took off my glasses and pinched the bridge of my nose. What the producer wanted . . . I would play her game this time but this contract better materialize soon. Friday at the dinner party, I was thinking. "I'm sure Reeve would be a big help. Renaissance Astrology, you say?"

"Yes. Renaissance Astrology."

"All right. I'll make this last call and then head on over."

After hanging up with Janelle, I phoned the final

agent on my list then rang up Reeve. "Hello, pretend boyfriend. Where are you right now?"

"Just going for a run with my friend Jill."

This news stoked a flare of jealousy in me. "Jill? Good mate, is she?"

He laughed. "She's a great mate. A great friend."

"How lovely," I said coolly, trying but failing to set aside this annoying envy.

Just focus on the job, Sutton.

"Is there a chance you could meet me at the public library on Fifth and Forty-Second in an hour?"

He was quick to answer. "I need to shower," he said. "So an hour from now, I might be naked . . ."

I drew in a sharp breath. The tease. The absolute tease.

"So better make it an hour and a half."

"Yes, let's do. Enjoy your run. And your shower."

There was a sound that might have been his chuckle. "I always do. Though even more when it's shared . . . You know. To conserve water."

With that little nudge, I was picturing Reeve in the shower. Maybe it was just as well that I got out of my office and into someplace full of books, art, and science—stimulation for the mind and less for the body.

14

REEVE

I was just following orders, and man, did she give them well.

"Gotta go," I told Jill as we ran down the West Side Bike Path.

She pouted. "Come on! You're the only one who can keep up with me. I thought we were going for eight miles today. You're going soft." She pushed my not-at-all-soft arm as we kept pace together.

I scoffed. "Ha. I could totally school you. But, one, I already did weights at the gym this morning, and two, I have to be somewhere."

"One, you can't school me. Two, where do you have to go? I thought you weren't working this week."

"Not at the messenger job, no. This is a side gig."

"And you were supposed to help me get ready for my *Crash the Moon* audition," Jill said. The midday sun beat down. It was November, and the air was chilly, but with five miles under our belts already, I felt pretty warm.

"I'll help you tomorrow," I said as we ran farther. "I have to cruise all the way over to the east side to shower, then get to Midtown."

She shot me a curious look. "Fine. Leave me, if you must, but don't leave me hanging. What's the gig? Who was that on the phone?"

I shook my head and laughed. We had just enough run left for me to tell Jill everything. As we slowed, her eyes widened, and then she punched me on the arm as if she were proud of me. "Can you get me an audition for *Escorted Lives*? I'd be happy to play a receptionist at the agency. Anything, anything at all."

I stopped running and kissed Jill quickly on the forehead. "You know I'll do whatever I can for you," I said, and I meant it. "You're my good mate."

She affected a British accent too. "Cheers, mate."

I waved goodbye, then I ran across town, showered, changed, and caught the subway to the New York Public Library where Sutton was waiting outside by the lions. Damn, she looked sharp in black leather boots, a short skirt, and a black coat cinched at the waist. All that luscious hair was pinned up again, and she had her glasses on. I couldn't stop my eyes from wandering to her legs, and just as I suspected, I saw the slightest hint of lace. Thigh-high stockings again. She was killing me.

Sadly, maddeningly, her smile was as plastic as it had been after the theater. That hard smile didn't go with the lace-tipped stockings. I couldn't read her.

She leaned in and gave me a kiss on the cheek.

I shook my head. Hell, no. That was not going to

do. "After six months together, all I get is a peck on the cheek?"

I placed my hands on her face and tilted it so her blue eyes met mine, and as I gazed at her, her pupils grew bigger and her walls started to melt away. Her body shifted the slightest bit closer, but I stayed totally still. I wanted her to feel the weight of my stare. I wanted her to feel undressed by my eyes, unwound by my touch.

And then, there it was. The slightest parting of her lips. I wasted no time, diving in for a deep and hungry kiss, right there on the front steps of the library as book borrowers and researchers and students and tourists streamed past on their way up or down. We were a postcard of kissing. We were the naval hero and his sweetheart reunited after he'd been at sea. We were lovers who couldn't keep their hands off each other after weeks apart.

We were every kiss on every street that anyone had ever gawked at and wished it was them being kissed like that.

Sutton moved against me, her chest lightly pressing against the cotton of my T-shirt beneath my scuffed leather jacket. Just when I felt her start to give in completely, I pulled away, grabbed her hand, and led her up the stairs.

Still wobbly from the kiss, she missed a step and stumbled. In one swift move, I grabbed her elbow then slid an arm around her waist.

"You okay?"

Her eyes were wide, the tiniest bit shocked. It

would only have been a small tumble. It would only have caused a minor scrape or bruise. Still, she seemed glad to have been caught.

"Thank you."

Then I stopped and gave her a soft kiss on her forehead. "I'm always happy to catch you."

It was just a thing to say. But hearing myself, I realized how earnestly I meant it. I was happy to be around her and even happier to be able to save her from even minor discomfort. It made me feel useful. It made me feel like there might be a way to get her to always look at me the way she did now.

15

SUTTON

That kiss.

He kissed me like it was the only thing that mattered in the world. I ran my fingers absently across my top lip as if I could feel the kiss still there. I wanted to revel in it. To live in it. To encase myself in that bubble of an afternoon kiss.

It wasn't fair. It wasn't fair in the least because it was all an act. Because he had the raw talent to pull that off, to make a kiss seem so convincing I'd suspended disbelief out there.

I had to restore the balance of power somehow, especially after the way I'd tripped. I was woozy and drunk from his kisses, so drunk I could barely walk straight. I had to right my ship. So as we wandered through shelves upon shelves of hardbound volumes on science and literature, on history and make-believe, I chatted in a low voice.

"So you took a degree in literature?" I asked as we rounded a corner on the way to Renaissance Astrology. The smell of musty old books was strong, and there was dust in the air. Nearby, quiet patrons worked on computers or slouched low in crackly leather chairs with their tomes, the pages lit by the faint glow of green lamps with pull-chain switches.

Reeve nodded. "Yep, American Lit. Ernest Hemingway. Ralph Ellison. Faulkner," he said, rattling off names. He paused, shaking his head. "Faulkner—definitely not a fan of."

"Why not?" I asked as I peered down a long row of books on—as promised—Renaissance Astrology. The wooden shelves were high, and no one was in the aisle. I tipped my head that way, and he followed.

"He made no sense," Reeve said about Faulkner. "You ever try to read him?"

I nodded. "All I remember is it felt like Yoda talking. Every sentence was written backward, it seemed."

Reeve laughed, and I liked the sound of his laughter. I liked, too, that I felt back in charge.

"But I'm definitely a fan of F. Scott Fitzgerald."

"Right. Of course. You said *Fear and Loathing in Las Vegas* and *The Great Gatsby* were toss-ups for your favorite book ever."

Reeve flashed a small smile at me as we reached the end of the aisle. I looked around. We were in a section of the library full of books on the most prominent constellations in the 1600s and what they portended.

Taking them all in, Reeve quoted in a sultry voice, "I've been drunk for about a week now, and I thought it might sober me up to sit in a library."

I cocked my head and looked at him curiously. "What is that?"

"Some dude says it in *The Great Gatsby* when Nick finds him in the library."

"Oh. How apropos," I said. There seemed to be a double meaning in the line—or perhaps it was the parallels to where we were. A library, the feeling of being drunk on kisses. Then there was the scene we were scouting for.

Or maybe my mind went straight to double-entendres around Reeve.

I felt that dryness in my throat again, and I swallowed.

"So I suppose you're a big fan of Jay Gatsby and Daisy Buchanan then?"

Reeve shook his head and leaned against the wooden panel of the shelves. "No. I think they're selfish pricks."

"Really? You don't hear that often."

He nodded intensely, his jaw ticking. "All they care about is themselves. They're held up as this great ideal of a doomed love affair, but they're totally self-centered. Daisy especially. She pretty much ignores her kid all the time." He scoffed derisively.

"I don't disagree with you, but it does raise the question. Why do you like the book then?"

"Easy," he said with a grin. "I like the writing. Lines like 'I love New York on summer afternoons when everyone's away. There's something very sensuous about it—overripe, as if all sorts of funny fruits were going to fall into your hands.'"

Listening to him quote sumptuous passages from literature in that sexy, smooth voice of his was not going to help me stay in control. My knees felt wobbly. I pressed a hand against my forehead as if I might faint.

"You okay?" he asked in a soft voice. Then he reached for me, brushing loose strands of hair across my forehead.

I nodded, afraid to speak. No other actor had ever affected me like this. It was much easier to say "I don't date actors" if no actor had ever tempted me before. They were work to me. They were my job. A job I loved, but that was all. Call them in, try them out, pick the best.

Reeve was far too skilled at playing the role of a man who loved me. He made me suspend disbelief too easily. Or maybe it was that I wanted so badly to believe him.

He looped his hands around my neck, drawing me nearer to him.

"I like the last line of the book too. 'Tomorrow we will run faster, stretch out our arms farther . . . And one fine morning—So we beat on, boats against the current, borne back ceaselessly into the past.'"

I inhaled sharply and damn near collapsed. This was too much. I was Silly Putty with him, I was a teenager touched for the very first time. There were sparks inside all the private places in my body, and I wanted him to know he put them there. I inched closer, and he drew his arms tighter around me.

"I see great writing turns you on, Sutton," he whispered, then left a soft kiss on my neck.

"You too," I said, and pressed against his jeans. He
was rock hard, and knowing I affected him made me
suddenly feel like I could turn the tables. Most of the
time, I felt so out of control, so much like an open
book, that I needed to get my power back before I fell
even further under the spell of his words, his tongue,
his fingers—those eyes that drowned me in desire.

This was how I'd regain the upper hand.

I pressed a palm against the denim of his jeans,
and he responded with a long, low moan. I grinned
wickedly. Oh yes, this was going to be fun.

Glancing one way, then another, I saw that no one
was near us. We were in the far corner of the stacks,
all alone on a Wednesday afternoon. I heard no foot-
steps, only the faint ticking of a wall clock somewhere
and then a low hum, likely a heater. We were
surrounded only by books, by the facts and fictions of
Renaissance men and women trying to map their lives
from the moon and the stars.

This man made me feel wild, unhinged. Might as
well be that wild woman.

"There's really only one way to know for sure if
this is the ideal location for the famous library scene,"
I said, feeling naughty as I began unzipping his jeans
and loving that feeling. I looked up at him, as if to ask
if it was okay. But I wasn't really asking. I just wanted
to see the surprise in his eyes, and yes, it was there. He
hadn't expected this. There was a little nervousness in
him right now. But as I reached my hand inside his

briefs, feeling the hard length of him, I knew he wouldn't back down.

He felt amazing—long and thick and sculpted. Velvet soft outside, rock hard inside. I could have spent all afternoon playing with him, toying with him, delighting in the perfection of his size. But there was work to be done, and orgasms to be achieved, and the clock was ticking. I kneeled, and keeping one hand wrapped firmly around the base, I kissed the tip. He let out another quiet moan, and when I glanced up, I saw him leaning back against the books, biting down hard on his lip.

I teased him for a few seconds with my tongue, and from the way he twined his fingers into my pinned-up hair, he enjoyed the feel of my lips on his long, hard length. I wanted to run my tongue from one side, then the other, tasting every inch. I wanted to savor his deliciousness and take my sweet time getting to know every fabulous inch of him. But instead, I wrapped my lips around him, and brought him all the way into my mouth.

He gripped my hair tighter as little sounds and moans escaped his lips. As I moved up and down, bringing him as far into my throat as I could, wanting him to feel completely surrounded by my warm, inviting mouth, I gazed up at him. His eyes were shut hard, and his features were screwed up in a look of exquisite pleasure. *At last.* I could do to him what he'd done to me. I could take charge of his pleasure. I could ensure that those waves of sweet release washed over him. I could have told him, "Don't worry.

I've got this," but I had a feeling he wasn't worried at all. Besides, my mouth was quite full.

I teased him all over with my tongue and my lips, pressing my hands against his strong, hard thighs—toned from all that cycling—for balance. He grabbed at my hair, and that aroused me more, knowing how close he was.

I wanted to touch myself at the same time. I was aching, longing desperately for him to lift me up so I could wrap my legs around him and slide onto him, riding him there in the library, fighting the desire to scream his name in pleasure. I was a loud one, and I never held back if I had a choice.

But this moment was for him. Because pleasing him would give me back my power. I wouldn't feel so helpless. He was a perfect specimen of hotness in every way, and I couldn't resist bringing him in deeper.

"Sutton," he moaned, and that made me tighten my lips around him. I loved that he was so far gone into the feeling that he had to say my name, he couldn't keep quiet. Soon, he rocked his hips into me, and I went faster, as more low and quiet moans met my ears. Then he thrust once, twice, and I tasted him for the first time, and I loved it. I wanted more of it, more of him. I could do this every day.

When he was done, I rose and brushed one hand against the other. Reeve had a dazed look etched across his gorgeous features.

"Why, yes, I think the Renaissance Astrology section will do just fine."

16

SUTTON

Later that night, I had just finished researching all the vital details on a rising filmmaker who'd requested a meeting with me next week. The filmmaker had nabbed top honors at Sundance and wanted to bring both marquee names and unknowns into his next project, a dramedy about a group of guy friends a few years after college. I placed my file and notes on my coffee table and poured a glass of chardonnay, allowing myself a few minutes to kick back.

With a wineglass in one hand, I wandered over to my bookshelves, scanning for a paperback I'd held on to since university. I took a sip of the chardonnay, then pulled the dog-eared book from the shelf and sank onto my soft couch, pulling a red chenille throw over my legs. The Artful Dodger hopped onto the sofa and curled up next to me, and I opened the book and turned to my favorite page. "Tomorrow we will run faster, stretch out our arms farther . . . And one fine morning—So we beat on, boats against the current, borne back ceaselessly into the past."

Was it kismet that he adored this line too?

A sign, maybe?

I ran my index finger over the line, letting the memories of this afternoon flash past. Reeve and his kiss. Reeve and the way he caught me on the steps. Reeve and his words "I'm always happy to catch you."

On the coffee table, my phone pinged with a text, and I placed the book on the couch and reached for it. It was from Reeve, and I would think it was odd, him texting as I was thinking about him, except that I thought about him so much, it was a statistical probability.

Opening the text, I tapped on the picture he must have taken that afternoon, right after we'd parted ways in front of one of the library's two stone lions.

He'd captured the steps leading into the building, on the exact spot where he'd kissed me and time had stopped and the world had begun spinning around us. The moment I came undone for him.

There was only one word with the photo. One word and one punctuation mark: *Encore?*

I ran my fingertip lazily across that message, as if the word itself made me feel all these tingles, even though it was the memory of Reeve's lips.

Encore. He was asking for a repeat performance. Not of what I'd done to him in the stacks, though I was sure he wouldn't mind another one of those, thank you very much.

But rather an encore of a show-stopping kiss.

I didn't answer his question. That would mean admitting how much I wanted another kiss like that. But curled up on the couch now, I did allow myself a reply: *"I am reading your favorite book right now."*

My finger hovered over the send button. If I sent this, I was choosing to engage. I was pressing beyond the physical and acting on the emotional. I would be getting to know him in a deeper way.

I hit send.

Moments later a reply arrived. *Tell me one of your favorite lines . . .*

I flipped through the book, easily finding another one. *"You won't like it, because it's about her."*

"Try me," he wrote back.

I tapped out another quote, one that tugged at my heart. *"There must have been moments even that afternoon when Daisy tumbled short of his dreams—not through her own fault but because of the colossal vitality of his illusion. It had gone beyond her, beyond everything. He had thrown himself into it with a creative passion."*

I took a sip of my wine, and soon Reeve's name reappeared, but it wasn't a text. He was calling.

I froze. Should I answer it? He knew I was around. Would he think I was avoiding him if I didn't pick up?

He'd be right. I couldn't fake my way out of this one.

"Hello there," I said in my best sparkly voice. I was never aware of my own British accent, but I'd been told that it made me sound both smart and aloof. Those were traits that might serve me well right now.

"I love that line too."

"Oh, you do?"

"Yes. I think it's about the ways we have these ideals of different things and people. Don't you? I mean, why do you love the line?"

I loved it because it was passionate, because it was big, because it was epic. But I wasn't prepared to say that, so I turned the question around. "Do you, Reeve? Have ideals about things and people?"

He paused before answering, and I wondered where he was. I heard music in the background, but from a stereo or home speaker, not a club. He must be at home. "Yeah. Of course. I'm sure I have this ideal about acting and theater and the craft, right? I kind of have to."

I was eager to learn more about the man. "Why? Why do you have to?"

"I just think you can't do this as a career if there's anything else you remotely can see yourself doing."

I nodded. "I believe that. I believe that about any type of art. Writer, painter, actor. It has to be the only thing for you."

"Right. And it's like that quote. It goes beyond her, beyond everything. It becomes everything."

Everything. I let that word resonate in the air around me. Actors loved acting first, best, and only. If I let my heart too far out of my chest, I'd have no one but myself to blame. Reeve might sound alluringly interested in this lovely getting-to-know-you phase right now, but that's because he was throwing himself into this role—the role of the boyfriend—in the only way he knew how. Wholeheartedly, and with a creative passion.

We were just that. A creation.

It wasn't kismet. It wasn't a sign.

This was yet another scene in the script of our relationship. And that was totally fine, right? I didn't really feel anything for him. It's not as if I was longing for this thing to extend beyond a week anyway.

I yawned, big and long and exaggerated. He might have been able to tell it was a fake yawn. But I needed an out, and it was the best I could do. "I'm sleepy. I better go. I'll see you tomorrow for a dress rehearsal, so to speak."

"See you tomorrow, Sutton," he said, then paused. "I can't wait."

I hung up, took a long swallow of wine, placed the drained glass on my coffee table, then made room for my main man, who curled up by my knees. I closed the novel and reached for my files, reminding myself that actors were part of my job, not part of my heart.

Even though I couldn't wait to see him too.

17

REEVE

The dinner was tomorrow. We had one more night of this pretend relationship, and I wanted to have all my lines down cold. I didn't want there to be any fuckups. But then, with what she'd done to me in the library and what I'd done to her in the theater, I couldn't imagine anyone would think we weren't a real couple. Fact was, we had chemistry in spades. There was something combustible between the two of us. It was as if I'd been given the keys to her body, and the same for her with me. As I walked to her apartment that evening on the Upper East Side, I was still thinking about the way we connected—but not just physically, because I liked talking to her too.

More than I'd expected.

Matter of fact, I'd never thought I'd be so into this arrangement. That I'd want more.

I rang the buzzer.

"Be right down," she said, and I waited on the steps of her brownstone.

I looked up and down her street. It was one of those quiet blocks in the Seventies, not far from the park. There were trees and pretty stoops, and brick buildings and lots of families pushing strollers or holding hands with young children. It was a far cry from where I lived down in the East Village in a tiny shoebox of an apartment that I'd snagged on a sublease when an actor buddy got a touring role in the German production of *Book of Mormon*.

But Sutton did well for herself, so it was no surprise she could handle a block like this. I leaned against the stone railing that led to her building, watching the street. A few fallen leaves blew past me, courtesy of the crisp autumn that had landed in Manhattan. I wore jeans, combat boots, and a T-shirt —this one with the words Unplug Electric Vampires in a cool white typewriter font. I had on my beat-up leather jacket, and I hadn't shaved, so my jaw was rough with a bit of stubble. I ran a hand through my hair, and turned when I heard Sutton say, "Hey you."

There was something sweet in her voice, something almost romantic. I'd never heard her talk that way before. I turned to watch her walk down the steps with her dog—a tiny little brown and tan mix with a cute face and a worn blue fleece jacket. But Sutton looked even better. I'd only seen her dressed up, and now I was getting a glimpse of the after-hours gal—she had on skinny jeans that showed off every gorgeous curve, short boots, and a jacket.

Then, as if she'd remembered that she didn't talk in sweet, lovey voices, she cleared her throat and returned to her all-business tone. "Hi there, Reeve. So glad you can join my little darling and me for a jaunt through the neighborhood."

But I liked it better when Sutton let down her guard, and I was curious about the softer side of this sharp and smart woman, so I tried to draw her back. "Your dog is kind of insanely cute." I kneeled down to pet the soft little guy.

"Thank you," she said, and there was that sweetness again, but as I rose to give her a kiss on the cheek —just in case anyone was watching, I reasoned—she was steely once more. Maybe *she* was the actress because I couldn't read her anymore. She had this mask on—as if she felt she needed to be friendly, smiling, witty Sutton with me, not the sweet one who melted under my touch.

I wondered where that Sutton had gone. But I didn't know what to say or how to ask, so I simply gestured to the sidewalk, and off we went, The Artful Dodger at the end of his leather leash, nose to the ground, sniffing and leading the way.

"Quite a fall we're having, isn't it?" she remarked.

This is what we were doing? Talking about the weather. "Yeah. It's definitely fall."

"So crisp. And the leaves are changing."

The sky was blue too. But I didn't need to point that out. "Yep. They are definitely changing."

"And soon winter will be here."

What had gotten into her? "That's usually how it goes. One follows the next," I said, not bothering to mask the sarcasm.

She gave me a sharp stare.

"And then spring, and then summer," I continued. "I studied the seasons in school." But I wasn't being playful. I was annoyed that she was being so . . . clinical . . . so cool.

"What a great school. And how was your day?" She knew exactly what I was doing, and exactly what she was doing. She wasn't going to let me in, and it pissed me off.

"It was whatever. I went for a run with Jill. Helped her get ready for her big audition next week."

"Oh, Jill. You helped her, did you?"

I smiled privately when I heard the jealousy in her voice. She couldn't hide it, and I was glad.

"Yeah. I help her with a lot of things," I added, and it was probably a stupid thing to add, but if I could get a rise out of Sutton, I'd take it.

"What sort of things?" she asked coldly as we walked past a shoe store peddling heels that cost half my monthly rent.

"This. That," I said in an offhand way, stirring the pot.

"Oh. *This. That,*" she repeated, punctuating each word.

"Why? Does it bother you?" I asked.

"Should it bother me?" Her expression was arch. Completely arch. And it drove me crazy.

"You're my fiancée. Why don't you tell me? As my fiancée, does it bother you?"

She didn't meet my gaze, so I couldn't even try to read her eyes. She stopped to let her dog sniff a small patch of grass surrounding a tree. "We're not real fiancés. We're not real anything. So there's no real way anything you do could bother me." She finished her summation on a too cheery note.

"Alright. That's clear, then," I said through tight lips. I stuffed my hands into the pockets of my jeans.

She held up a finger. "Wait. There is one thing you could do that would bother me. It would bother me if you blew the deal. So don't do anything with Jill or anyone until we finalize things, okay? Then you're free to go," she said, chipper again.

I scoffed at her, then held my hands out wide. "That is very good to know. Very good to know, indeed."

"Anyway, let's go over tomorrow night's dinner and how you need to behave," she said as we reached the crosswalk and waited for the light. She pointed one finger at The Artful Dodger, and he sat instantly. The dog was well-trained, and that's what Sutton was all about. Training me. That's who she was. Bright and shiny on the outside, cool and calculating on the inside.

We walked for several more blocks, and she reviewed the ins and outs, the expectations, the potential questions, until our fake relationship was airtight and hermetically sealed. She was the instructor and I was the pupil, and she wasn't going to let me forget it. As we turned back toward her apartment, she issued her final directive. "And of course, you should feel free to touch me. Hand on the leg, hand on the arm. Holding hands, kiss on the cheek.

All of that is totally acceptable," she said, then shot me that smile I'd come to recognize as her "thank you very much, we'll be in touch" look.

Then there was a scuffle of paws. The rattle of a chain collar. Out of nowhere, a big, brown German Shepherd barreled down the sidewalk, snarling at the little Artful Dodger. His teeth were bared, and his nostrils were flaring, and he was off the leash. The German Shepherd's mouth was open, and he had one thing in mind. Evening snack.

Sutton shrieked.

Instantly, I lunged through wiry fur and snapping teeth for the bigger dog, grabbing the prong collar as hard as I could and yanking the German Shepherd away from The Artful Dodger. The big dog growled and whipped his head around, unveiling sharp teeth that looked as if they could sink holes into skin. But I held on tight to the chain on the dog's neck, even as the German Shepherd scraped his jaw against my wrist trying to twist loose. Then with my free hand, I scooped up the tiny pup, tucking him under my arm, like a football being cradled by a running back. The pony-sized dog yanked and tugged, and for a second I thought my arm was about to be tattooed with a set of dog bite marks, then I heard a voice call out.

"Henry! Henry! You bad dog!"

The shepherd cocked his ears and wagged his tail and was suddenly a sweet, doting animal searching for his person. A dude in loose jeans, ballcap, and sweatshirt rounded the corner, a look of surprise on his face. In one hand, he held a nylon leash. He ran to the German Shepherd and stopped.

"I'm so sorry. We just got him, and he has some issues, but we're trying to train him."

"Some issues? He almost killed our dog," I said, tucking the shivering little guy more tightly in my arms.

The man looked legit contrite. "I'm really sorry."

Even so, that dog needed to be leashed and this guy needed to know. "You have to be more careful. There are kids and other dogs and people every-where, okay? He was about to bite our dog."

"Okay, I said I was sorry."

I relaxed a bit. But only a little because I was still pissed. "Yeah. So good luck with the training."

The guy clipped the leash back onto Henry and pulled him the other way. I turned to Sutton who stared at me, eyes wide and mouth agape. "You saved my dog."

I passed him into Sutton's outstretched arms, downplaying it.

"He'd have been fine. He's a tough little guy."

Sutton shook her head, her voice quivering, as she clutched the dog. "I can't believe you did that. You were so fast," she said breathlessly, a tear slipping down her cheek. "You just reached your hand in there. He bit you. That dog bit you."

I was tough. I could handle it. "It's nothing. I swear it's nothing."

"Let me see." Sutton reached for my wrist,

touching tenderly around the red indentation from a canine tooth.

"There isn't even any blood. I'm totally fine."

She was insistent. "We should get this cleaned up."

"Sut, it's nothing. I swear I'm totally fine."

"Please." She looked so pleading, so warm again. This was what I had wanted. Not to be bitten, or to be nursed and fretted over—because the mark she was so concerned about was barely a graze. But I wanted this Sutton. The one beneath the veneer.

"How about this? I'll let you buy me a drink."

18

SUTTON

I absolutely owed him a drink, or ten, but I didn't want to leave my darling alone, so we popped into a bodega for a beer for Reeve then went back to my place where I poured a white wine for myself. The Artful Dodger was safe and sound, snoozing in the middle of the king-size bed, surrounded by extra blankets to make him a cozy nest.

As it should be.

I was still shaken, and shaking. The whole thing had happened so fast, and I'd go a long time before I lost the memory of my darling dog almost becoming a snack for that German Shepherd.

And Reeve. I hardly knew what to think. He hadn't even hesitated. And his reflexes—I was still wrapping my head around the way he dove into the melee and saved my most favorite mammal in the entire universe.

We sank into the soft couch in my living room, drinks in hand.

"I can't thank you enough," I said again, setting a hand on his arm, squeezing it. "I don't say this lightly, but you are my hero."

His smile was warm and genuine. "I'm just glad he's fine. He's a good dog, and he's your dog." He took a sip of his beer then confessed, "Actually, I hope this doesn't make me less of your hero, but I'd help save any dog."

Less of my hero? Just the opposite. He loved animals. My heart was in a race with the electricity zipping through me just being this close to him.

Careful, Sutton, careful. That was my tender spot, the gap in my armor—a man who loved animals. If Reeve figured that out, I'd be helpless.

I took a drink and placed my glass on the table. "That actually makes me even happier to know it wasn't just my dog. But that you're a dog superhero."

He preened, puffing out his chest. "That's me. Saving small pooches in a single bound." He tipped back his beer bottle, took a swallow, then set it down.

"All the Fidos in New York will sing your praises. They'll build rawhide monuments and bark your name with reverence for years to come."

"What more can a guy ask for? I've always wanted to be adored by mutts."

"There is nothing better to aspire to," I said, enjoying this casual conversation, the shift in our chatter, the way we could easily segue to different topics and have fun with each other.

"And hey," he added, "look on the bright side. Now we have another story to tell tomorrow night that'll make this"—he gestured from himself to me—"seem all the more real."

Real. There was that word again. This wasn't real, but it had felt so real during the dog walk. I'd felt *real* jealousy over Jill. And I'd felt *real* admiration for Reeve when he saved my dog.

And then there was the way I felt right now.

Real feelings.

Damn.

I wanted to berate myself. To remind my idiotic heart that we teetered on the edge of a first-class mistake. Because this was the thing I'd most wanted to avoid. I'd never intended to let him into my heart. He was acting, only acting. Somehow, the act had worked on me, and now I had fallen into feelings.

Because of that, because I don't do things by half-measures, I came out and asked the question that had been gnawing at me most of the afternoon. "Is there something with you and this Jill?"

He tilted his head back and laughed, showing off those brilliant straight white teeth.

I did not appreciate being laughed at. My shoulders tensed and squared up. I reached for my glass again just to give my hands something to do. "You don't have to laugh at me. It's a natural question, considering how much you talk about her."

He moved closer and pressed one strong hand on top of both of mine. "Because you are a conundrum."

He was the pot calling the kettle black, but I couldn't quite let on, so I acted shocked. Because, well, I was a little shocked. Was I not an open book to him?

"Me? How could I possibly be a conundrum?"

His eyes narrowed, not mad, but speculative. "Why do you want to know about Jill? You already told me how I had to act, and I'll do that."

All right, maybe a little mad.

But so was I. "I'll take that as a yes," I said in a clipped voice. "That you're involved with her." I felt a flash of anger toward him when I thought of the library and the theater.

"You're cheating on her," I said through gritted teeth. "Cheating on your girlfriend with me."

He laughed again and I tightened my fist. "No. I'm not. I've never cheated on anyone. I never would. When I'm with someone, I'm only with that someone." He didn't lose his smile, but he did catch my gaze and hold it, so I saw his sincerity. "That includes when I'm with her because of a business-adjacent agreement."

I should comment on "business-adjacent." How could it be "adjacent" when we were both doing our actual businesses? But what came out was a question, both petulant and hopeful. "So she's not your girlfriend?"

Reeve picked up his beer bottle, took a long drink, and set it back down, all while I ran my index finger along the rim of my wineglass. I was edgy, waiting. I waited until I couldn't stand it anymore. "Reeve, just tell me."

He grinned like he'd won a prize, like this was

where he'd been headed all along with his teasing. "No, Sutton. She's a great, great friend. We like each other, as buddies. So don't worry. I've never done the things to her that I've done to you."

Heat flared in my belly, and my skin warmed. I liked the sound of that. I wanted more of that. "What do you mean?"

He moved closer and draped an arm around my shoulders. I loved the warm, protective feel of his arm around me. The possessive way he looked at me. "I mean, I've never gotten her off in a theater. Or anywhere. I've never kissed her on the steps of the library. And she's never gone down on me in the stacks. Incidentally, you give a fucking awesome blow job."

He traced a finger lazily across my top lip, and I was speechless. I wasn't sure if he was playing the role again, the part he'd been hired for. Because he'd been pissy and irritated on the walk, but now he was flirty and sexy again. I didn't know what to make of it. But I knew I wanted to take his finger and suck on it. Then he pulled his hand away.

"But you never answered my text," he said, now annoyed.

"What do you mean?" I asked, trying to play it cool, but inside I was burning. "I replied to it."

He stared at me, hardness in his eyes. "Yeah, about a book. But you didn't answer the question. Encore? Do you want an encore?"

My God, of course I did. I wanted him so much. In

so many ways. In ways that went well beyond the physical. "For real?"

"Yes. And I'll show you."

Somewhere inside me, I let a piece of my heart free for a moment, and it felt fabulous. Did this mean he was catching feelings too? I didn't have time to ponder the question because his lips were on mine again. He explored my mouth, tenderly at first, then rougher as if he wanted to consume me. I responded in kind, grabbing at his hair, silky smooth between my fingers, pressing one hand against his firm chest and bringing his mouth closer and deeper as if every life and breath depended on this kiss. I wanted him to devour me.

He broke the kiss and looked at me.

"Damn, woman. You like being kissed, don't you?"

I blushed and looked away, embarrassed. I hated that I was this way with him. So easy. One touch and I was ready to go. One quick kiss and I was about to spread my legs right here.

"Hey," he said, softly. He pressed a palm on my cheek and turned my face back to him. "I like kissing you. I like being the one you want to kiss. I mean it."

"You do?"

He nodded. "Yes. I want to kiss you in other places too."

"Where else . . .?" I whispered. The way he looked at me with those deep brown eyes, the way he talked to me, the way he touched me—I was liquid heat with barely a word, with merely a touch.

"I want to kiss your neck," he said, then leaned in to plant a soft, sweet kiss on my neck.

"And your earlobe looks pretty tasty." He nibbled lightly on my earlobe, then swept his tongue up my ear. I shivered as he went.

"And this spot," he said, touching the hollow of my throat. "I bet you'd like being kissed there too."

"I would," I whispered, and he brushed his lips gently there. I breathed deeply, my breasts rising and falling, and he stole the chance to cup them quickly.

Then he pulled back. "There too. Your breasts. I would very much like to take them in my mouth. Well, you know, not at the same time," he said, playfully and I laughed. "But if I could, I would. Because I want to taste your nipples and swirl my tongue across the flesh of your breasts. First one, flicking my tongue over your nipple, then bringing as much of your delicious flesh into my mouth as I could. Then the other."

My breasts ached with the need to be touched. "Please," I whispered.

He did as I asked. I closed my eyes and sighed. He pulled me closer, cupping me through my thin gray sweater, feeling the points on my nipples grow hard. He moved his mouth to my ear and whispered, "But there are so many other places to kiss you, Sutton."

"Yes," I said on a moan, as a haze spread over me from his touch.

"You need to be kissed on your belly. From your ribs, down to your belly button, and over to your hips. And you need to be kissed on your legs. On the back of your calves, and inside your thighs." His voice was gravelly and so damn sexy, his hands eagerly mapping where he'd kiss me.

"I want all that."

He dusted his lips across my neck. "Do you want me to kiss you all over your gorgeous body?"

I trembled with desire. "Yes," I whispered, feeling bare, telling him my truth.

He kissed the other side of my neck, turning me liquid. I was melting with this man, and helpless to stop it. His voice rumbled against my skin. "Tell me. Tell me where you want my lips."

Everywhere.

I didn't tell him. Instead, I showed him, taking his hand and pressing his palm against the fabric of my jeans. I was sure he could feel the heat radiating from my core. I was molten. I was a volcano for him. I felt as if I would shatter any second. All he had to do was talk to me, tell me all the things he'd do and I'd break in ecstasy.

He groaned as he cupped me through my jeans. "You do want me everywhere," he said, rough and sexy.

I whispered a yes.

My face was red with heat. My mouth was dry. I could barely speak. He was doing it again. He was stripping me of all pretensions, he was tearing down all the ways I'd tried to protect myself. He was a chemical reaction to me, the thing I couldn't resist.

He laid me back on the couch. His eyes locked with mine. "You want me to take off your jeans?"

"Yes," I murmured, wanting to speed up time.

He unzipped my jeans and pulled them off.

His lips curved in a crooked grin, as he held up my jeans in one hand. "And throw them on the floor of your apartment?"

I smiled, loving his naughty and funny side in this moment. "By all means."

He tossed my jeans.

Dirty deeds flashed across his eyes as he returned to me, his gaze roaming up and down my body, landing on my knickers. He ran a finger across the fabric, and I arched, then moaned.

"And pull off your panties?"

"Please, yes, now," I said in a broken whisper.

He slid them off me, a rumble coming from his chest as he stared at me. "Fuck, Sutton. You're gorgeous," he said as he stared.

When he finally touched me, I cried out so loudly I worried my faithful pooch would come trotting out to see what was wrong.

But he was a good boy, and I was not a good girl at all.

I was anything but, relishing this moment as Reeve placed his hands on my thighs and spread my legs.

He dropped his mouth to my wetness, and I lifted my hips, gasping and moaning and giving myself to him.

As he licked and kissed and sucked, desire pounded through my body. I was pulsing with the need for him, the need to be tasted, to be touched, to be devoured.

He murmured as he worked his magic tongue on

me, kissing, licking, flicking as he drove me wild. My pitch rose, my cries reverberated across the apartment, and my hands speared deep into his hair. His name was on my lips as I unraveled, falling apart as I rocked shamelessly against his face.

When I came down from the utter bliss, I was struck with the intensity of what I felt for him, with a wave of unexpected emotions.

He looked at me hungrily, but with something new in his eyes too. Something new and . . . maybe something *more*.

My heart stuttered then skipped.

Bloody hell.

Maybe this was only wishful thinking. Was I imagining the look in his eyes, hoping it mirrored mine?

And more—was I a fool to think it might be there?

I didn't know, had no clue, so I asked him a question where I was certain I knew the answer. "Can I do that to you?"

His grin was filthy, and I loved it.

Almost as much as I loved giving him the same treatment, hearing his sounds, hearing him call my name.

And the absolutely insane thing was, I was sure, I was hearing it in a new way.

With reverence. With something like adoration.

That was silly. So silly.

I couldn't let myself imagine such things were happening.

So I yawned, claimed I was exhausted, and told him I needed to go to bed.

He left, pressing a kiss to my forehead that felt a little bit like a goodbye.

It couldn't be, because we still had the dinner tomorrow.

Or maybe it was.

* * *

The only thing to do now was talk to a friend, so I texted McKenna.

Sutton: I'm simply going to say it for you and save you the trouble. You told me so.

McKenna: I've told you a lot of things. What was it this time?

Sutton: I think I'm falling for my fake fiancé.

McKenna: That should be the title of your next movie.

Sutton: Not funny. I mean, it kind of is, but I'm obliged not to laugh.

McKenna: It is funny. And I'll remind you of that when it's a big hit. You heard it here first . . .

19

REEVE

I was nervous about tonight's dinner, but I wasn't sure why.

I always got a little nervous before I went on stage, and I supposed this counted. When I was acting, I used that nervous energy to fuel my performance. Nerves made me sharp, they made me go deeper into the character. The more nerves I felt, the easier it was to let go of myself when I stepped on stage and the more easily I immersed myself in the role I was playing.

I headed over to Jill's place in Chelsea, needing to talk to someone who understood those feelings, and because spending time with friends always centered me, and that's what I needed. Centering. Balance. Calm.

Jill buzzed me in, and I bounded up the steps to the second-floor apartment, the soles of my combat boots smacking the concrete in the stairwell. I'd barely reached her door when Jill flung it open for me.

"How's my favorite boy toy?" she asked with a knowing grin.

I held out my hands in a what-can-I-say shrug, putting a satisfied smile on my face. And I *was* satisfied, but I was kind of a wreck too. Those emotions I was burying deep, though, because they weren't normal nerves before a performance, and because I needed to get in character. I had a part to play, and I didn't want to let Sutton down.

After last night, I wasn't sure where things stood with us. While I'd been with Sutton in her apartment, I'd have answered it easily -- said *great, terrific, amazing*. I did to her everything I promised, and then some, plus gotten plenty in return. Oh hell, did she ever give back.

For a moment there last night, maybe many, it had felt like we were on the cusp of something more. Now, I was simply holding tight to the memory of her coming apart for me to use it as a touchstone for what I wanted things to be. Because we weren't there now. As I'd walked home last night, I hadn't felt at all like a man who'd just had fantastic sex.

That was the trouble.

That was still the trouble.

I'd felt like a man who'd wanted to stay but had been kicked out.

Huh. Maybe this was, actually, what an escort felt like. Being intimate—feeling intimate—and then getting hustled out the door.

Though, Sutton had shut her door before she'd shown me out. After I'd sent her into the stratosphere, something shifted. She flipped the switch and her walls came back up with me on the outside. And it sucked.

Jill waved a hand in front of my face. "Earth to Reeve."

"Oh." I blinked. "Sorry. I was . . ."

"Drifting off and imagining how fabulous your special assignment is?"

I sighed heavily. Because this had become more than an assignment. More than I'd expected or prepared for. More than I had braced for.

When the utterly unforeseen happens, only one thing is good for that. I needed carbs and sugar. Fine, two things. But they came in one perfect form. "Let's go get some pancakes," I said.

Jill stared at me, joking put aside. "This is a Code Pancake? You should have said that right away."

I scrubbed a hand across my jaw. "I'm not sure I realized it right away. But I sure as hell do now."

She squeezed my arm gently. "Maybe you need to catch me up on what's happened."

"Can I tell you while we walk to the diner?" I asked, eager for my carb fix now. And my friend fix.

"Code Pancake indeed. I'll grab my jacket," Jill said, and we were out the door in seconds in hot pursuit.

As we made our way to a cheap nearby diner, I filled Jill in on the basics of the night before. I didn't go into elaborate detail, but she got the gist, and I finished about the time we settled into a booth. "So first date she sent me home in a taxi, this time I got kicked to the curb while she got a good night's sleep. I can't tell what she's thinking, or which Sutton I'll be getting—the sweet and sassy one or the casting director." I shrugged out of my jacket, tossing it next to me. "Maybe she's the player. Maybe she's just playing me for sex."

Jill wiggled her brows. "And that bothers you because . . .?"

"It doesn't bother me," I insisted, but I barely got the words out before I trailed off.

Jill's eyes went wide and she covered her mouth with her hand in exaggerated shock. Probably exaggerated. Maybe exaggerated. "You have fallen for Sutton Brenner."

Hearing her say it grounded me. Anchored me. Reminded me of what I'd realized on the way over. As the waitress took Jill's order, then mine, my mind wandered to the woman I was desperate to understand.

Food ordered, Jill stared expectantly at me. "So life as a man for hire isn't all peaches and sunshine?"

Briefly, I considered the perfectly valid tactic of denial. I could pull off the act. Being an actor and all. I could say *no, it's great, and I love it.*

But I'd gone to Jill for a reason, more than just a Code Pancake partner.

I was on edge, and I knew then it wasn't just nerves about tonight.

It was because, holy hell, Jill had called it—I was falling for Sutton Brenner.

Hook, line and fake fiancé sinker.

I took a deep breath. "It seems life is imitating art. I'm supposed to be in love with Sutton, and I've been seeing more why someone—why *I*—would do that." With a shrug to deflect, I commented on my own situation. "Pretty ridiculous, right?"

She stretched her hand across the table, squeezing mine. "No." She paused, smiled softly. "You care for her. For real. Don't you?"

I swallowed roughly, flashing back to the last few days—had it only been that long? It felt like much longer . . .

"She's great, Jill. Hard to read sometimes—a lot of the time—but the glimpses of the sweet, sassy woman tell me she'd be worth the work. She's caring and kind. Smart as a whip and funny too. I didn't expect her to be funny. But she is. She has this dry, clever sense of humor." I glanced at Jill, realizing I was gushing but not sure I cared. "She has this adorable little dog she's nuts about, and I think she's the truest version of herself when she's around him. I kind of love watching who she is with that pooch. She tries to be tough, but she's such a marshmallow."

Sighing happily, Jill set her chin in her hands, batting her eyes. "Aww. She's your marshmallow."

I tried to laugh it off. But maybe that's what she was.

My marshmallow.

Our pancakes arrived, and I took the chance while our mouths were full to think of how I might tip the scales toward sweet Sutton tonight. She'd be warm in public, so there was that to enjoy. But what could I do for her to show I paid attention to her needs —the big one was making our charade convincing but also special for her tonight.

Then I remembered what Jill's roommate Kat did for a living. She was a jewelry designer. "Hey, Jill. Think your roommate can do me a favor?"

20
————

SUTTON

I sent a car to pick up Reeve. I knew if I saw his apartment, I'd start to feel more for him, and I couldn't allow that. The week was nearly up and we could soon return to passing acquaintances. Fine, he was an acquaintance who hit notes on my body that had never been played before. He'd gone down on me the night before and delivered two out-of-this-world orgasms that made me feel as if the sun and moon and solar system were rotating around me, that the sheer wattage of pleasure he'd given me with his mouth and tongue and lips could power the universe.

Still, I'd simply have to tuck him into the faraway corner of my brain after tonight. But his prowess with my body wasn't the most unjust part of this whole week. The real rub was this—he was sweet, and he was good, and he could keep up with me. He was his own man, with his own opinions, and he wasn't afraid of a thing.

There were times when he seemed to genuinely

care for me, and there were times when he touched me in a way that went beyond the intense charge between us. The way he'd kissed me on the library steps with a kind of reverence, as if he'd missed me. And the way he'd laid me down on my couch and spread my legs as if he were hungry for me, not just my body, but me.

I waved my hand in front of my face, as if I could rid myself of these ludicrous notions, then I appraised myself one last time in the mirror. I had on a pretty dove gray dress with long sleeves and a hemline that hit just above the knees. Then my black leather boots, and a single silver bracelet on my right wrist. I'd pinned my hair up as usual, and I wore my glasses, my twin efforts to look twenty-eight, rather than the twenty-one I was often mistaken for. I looked sophisticated and sharp, and when the town car arrived with Reeve already in the back seat, so handsome in his charcoal slacks, green button-down, and a tie, I felt a surge of happiness at seeing my boyfriend.

Then I remembered he was only my pretend boyfriend, so I tamped it down. "You look very nice," I said to him.

"As do you. And look," he said, tipping his forehead to a plate on the seat next to him, full of chocolate chip cookies covered in saran wrap. "Remember I told her in your office I made great chocolate chip cookies?"

I beamed. "You are the perfect boyfriend."

He winked. "They might not be as good as

Sunshine Bakery cookies, but I think they can hold their own."

I clasped my hand to my chest. "You go to Sunshine Bakery?"

He patted his belly. It was flat as a board. "From time to time. Gotta keep in shape for the camera, but I love that place."

A shiver of possibility raced over my skin. "It's my favorite too. Did you know they have grapefruit macarons?"

His lips twitched up in a grin. "Be still my beating heart. I'll have to take you there sometime." His voice lowered to a naughty whisper. "Then we'll work it off."

That shiver turned to heat, warming me all over. But I had to remind myself this was only pretend. "Count me in," I said, in my best sexy and nonchalant tone.

"And I have something for you," he added.

I raised an eyebrow curiously, as he removed from his pocket a small velvet pouch, then reached inside. Something sparkled in his hand, and it looked almost like a diamond. My eyes widened, and I let that joyful feeling return. I did love shiny objects.

"It's just a little something. It's not a real diamond, and I'm not trying to claim it's real, but I thought we could pretend it's a placeholder ring while you get yours resized." He held the ring in his palm and with his other hand, he reached for me.

My heart skipped a beat as he slid the ring onto

my finger. "Oh, Reeve. I love it. How did you get it? It fits perfectly."

He shrugged sheepishly. "I'm actually pretty good with sizes. It's this strange hidden talent of mine. And my friend Jill's roommate is a jewelry designer, so she knocked this out for us."

"This is ridiculously perfect," I said, and placed my bejeweled hand on the back of his head and planted a quick kiss on his lips.

A fake kiss, of course. It was only a fake kiss to get in the right mindset. But the way he lingered softly, the way he sighed happily, made it feel real.

Then I settled back in the leather seat and we said little more on the short drive to the penthouse apartment on Fifth Avenue. We didn't say much in the elevator either. I knocked on the door, and Janelle answered.

"Good to see you," Janelle said, letting the tiniest sliver of a smile slip across her slick red lips. She wore a maroon dress with a high neck and for a moment I wondered if Janelle was hiding hickeys. Then, I remembered that Janelle had supposedly cut Johnathan off till he proved he could keep it in his pants. But rather than ruminate on the sleeping arrangements of this woman, I handed her the bottle of Cakebread Chardonnay I'd selected from the local wine shop on my block.

"It's a 2011. It's supposed to be wonderful, so I very much hope you enjoy it."

"Oh, I'm sure I will," Janelle said, waving us inside the penthouse.

"And here are the cookies as promised," Reeve said, handing her the plate of baked goods.

"I cannot wait to eat them." She plucked one from under the Saran wrap and popped it into her mouth. She rolled her eyes in pleasure, then whispered. "Best. Ever."

Reeve smiled.

"Let me just put this wine in the wine cellar," Janelle added. "Though, it's not really a cellar. It's more of a closet. But I still call it a cellar. Come with me. I'll show it to you."

Janelle escorted us to the spacious kitchen, which itself was the size of my whole apartment. There was an island, a massive Viking stove, and a huge Sub-Zero built-in refrigerator. As Janelle placed the cookies on the island, the Siamese cat sashayed by.

"Hello, Archibald," I said to the feline. As felines do, he ignored me and wandered into another room.

"He's a cat," Janelle said, as if that explained everything. And it did.

It also occurred to me that Janelle was a cat kind of person. There were people who were dog people—accepting, unable to hide their emotions, announcing their preferences sometimes VERY LOUDLY. Then there were cat people—aloof, inscrutable, and most interested in you when you don't want them to be.

That summed Janelle up pretty well. It also explained why she looked like she was sneering even when she wasn't.

Janelle led us to an oak door that opened into a long narrow hallway full of bottles of wine. The lights were low in the wine cellar-slash-closet and the temperature was cooler. I shivered, and Reeve placed an arm around me. His touch was warm, and I leaned briefly into it.

Janelle placed the wine in a rack, and then gestured as if she were presenting winning letters on a game show. "Voila. And here it is. In case you should need to find it later." Then she whispered, as if we were in on something, "It's fun for all sorts of things."

"Um . . . right, then." I wasn't sure how to respond, so I kept my reply on the level. "Lovely. Great. We'll know right where to find it if we need wine. Or, um, a cellar."

We headed back to the main living area. As we went, Janelle asked idly. "Oh, by the way, I keep meaning to ask. How was Renaissance Astrology?"

By the way? As if that was an afterthought.

I looked quickly at Reeve, who smirked knowingly. There might be blow jobs that were afterthoughts, but that wasn't one of them.

"I think it's going to work out just fine for that scene. Just fine indeed," I said with a private grin.

"Really? Are you sure?" Janelle pressed.

I cut my gaze her way, trying to figure out her angle. "Yes. I'm quite sure."

Janelle smirked, and I realized—with my cat person insight—that was just the way she smiled. "And what did you think, Reeve?"

"Me?" The question surprised him, and he glanced at me then back at Janelle.

"You're the right type for the part," she said. "For a

number of roles in the movie, actually. Give us your perspective as the character. Is it *just fine?*

Reeve eyed her with understanding he'd better explain to me later. "I don't know if I'd say *just* fine." He draped his arm a bit possessively over my shoulders. "Let's just say, we are one hundred percent positive that it's the perfect location." He winked at Janelle, and leaned into me, dusting a kiss on my cheek. "Aren't we, babe?" he said to me.

He knew how to handle Janelle. How to play her, so I made a choice to trust him. "Yes, we are."

As Janelle walked into the living room, Reeve pulled me aside and spoke in a low voice.

"I think she might be a bit like the woman who runs the escort agency in *Escorted Lives.*"

"No. Really?" I resisted the urge to look over my shoulder after her.

Reeve didn't resist at all, but peered over my shoulder to make sure no one was in earshot.

"I'm betting," he whispered, "she's kind of a voyeur herself."

"No," I laughed, then stopped laughing because I didn't believe it but it wasn't really funny. "Impossible. No one with a bun that tight could be so . . ." Words failed me.

"People with buns that tight are exactly who you have to watch out for. What are they holding back so tightly?"

"Reeve," I said in my don't-be-foolish Mary Poppins voice, "consider the sheer weight of gossip about the Pinkertons. And think about what a small world the theater is. Movies too. Is there any way something like that wouldn't be some kind of mythic rumor?"

"Like Bigfoot?"

"Don't make me laugh, Reeve! It's going to be hard enough looking at her without washing my brain."

He raised his hands in surrender, his eyes dancing like he was the one with the secret—only mischievous, not pervy. Well, not pervy in a bad way.

God, I was never going to get through dinner.

Reeve and I joined the Pinkertons in the living room, where Nicholas and Johnathan sat like puffy buffoons on an antique-looking couch. We made small talk for the next hour as a caterer circled by offering hamachi, prosciutto-wrapped asparagus, and stuffed mushrooms. Then it was time for dinner, and we moved to the dining room, which boasted a gorgeous view of Central Park, wide and expansive from the tenth floor penthouse. Once again, Janelle stationed herself next to Reeve, much as she had at the theater. Did Janelle have a crush on Reeve? Well, if she did, I couldn't blame her. But if that woman tried to steal my boyfriend, I'd claw her eyes out.

Wait. Fake boyfriend. If Janelle tried to steal my fake boyfriend . . . *Oh, never mind.*

At the table, we chatted about movies and golf and the pending wedding, and once again Reeve rose to the occasion answering all sorts of questions without a moment's hesitation. It didn't take long for things to get more personal than our preferences in venues and cake flavors.

"And how did you know, Reeve? How did you know that Sutton was the one for you?" The question came from Nicholas's wife across the table.

Reeve turned his attention my way. "How did I know?" he asked, gazing at me as if he were contemplating the answer. "I'll tell you how I knew. Because there was no way I could *not* know. It couldn't be otherwise. I'd fallen hard for this woman from the moment I first met her, and the more I got to know her, the more I liked her."

"Oh, that is so sweet," Nicholas's wife said.

"Tell us more," Janelle chimed in.

I looked at the two wives. They seemed to be hanging on every word Reeve said to me. It was as if he was romancing them through me. Maybe that's what they wanted—to feel loved vicariously by a gorgeous, thoughtful young man. I understood that sort of wish. I wanted it too. Wished for a different situation. One where Reeve was not acting.

He went on. "Every day it became clearer how much there was to love. It's the way she takes care of her dog, and the way she teases me. It's the books she likes and her wry sense of humor. It's the way she appreciates all the things I do for her. It's the way she lets me save her when she needs saving. And the way she takes charge when she needs to take charge. It's the way she's so tough on the outside, but I can see through her and I know what's in her soft, sweet heart. And it's in the way she says yes." He nodded like making up his mind about something. "Most of all, it's the way she says yes."

I placed a hand on my belly, as if I could quell all the feelings, all the emotions, all the desire he'd stirred in me, saying those things, even here in front of everyone. I wanted to throw my arms around his neck and smother him in kisses. Forget all the make-believe. I was ready to go all in.

But yet, I knew better. I had to guard my heart. I had to be strong. I must refuse to let myself be seduced by the act.

I opened and closed my hands in my lap as he kept doing his job so very well.

"And I guess, most of all, it's that she chose me. She's the kind of woman who could have anyone, but she chose me," Reeve said as he looked deeply into my eyes.

I forced myself to feel nothing as he held my gaze, even though I felt everything for him. Every. Single. Thing. And it was killing me.

"So really," he said, "when you find someone you're crazy about, you don't let her go, right?"

Janelle clasped a hand on her mouth. She looked as if she were about to cry happy tears. "I think I need more wine," she said.

Johnathan started to get up, and she said "No!" Everyone at the table blinked, but she recovered quickly. "I mean, no Johnathan *dear*. Sutton and Reeve brought a fabulous bottle with them tonight." She turned to the both of us, but mostly Reeve, unless I missed my guess. "Would you mind fetching it from the cellar?"

"No problem," Reeve said and stood up, holding out a hand to me. I took it and followed him.

My knees wobbled, another sign of how much Reeve's in-love act had affected me. A warning about how vulnerable I was to him.

I was so angry with myself for not keeping my guard up, and even though he was only doing his job, pouring on the charm, convincing everyone that he loved me, irrationally, I was angry with him for not holding back. For not making it easier to remember he was acting.

21

REEVE

Sutton's heels clicked on the floor as we went down the hall Janelle had shown us, and her back was poker straight. I didn't want to borrow trouble but that didn't seem like a good sign. Her emotions were up, but not in the way I'd have wanted or expected after I'd poured my heart out that way.

Once inside the wine closet-slash-cellar, Sutton started looking for the wine we'd brought. For a moment, she didn't say anything, but then she said in a clipped tone, "That was quite a performance. I'm impressed. Even better than I'd expected, and my hopes were pretty high."

Her voice had layers hiding layers, and I didn't understand the half of them, but especially the sarcasm. "That's what you wanted, right?"

"Absolutely," she said. Her search for the wine bottle slowed, but it seemed now to be just an excuse to not look at me. "I wanted a good act, and you sold it." She paused, and said in a different, softer tone, "It was all an act, wasn't it?"

"Totally. Because you know what I'd have said if I'd told the truth?" I took her arm, turning her around so she was facing me, wine bottles on either side of us.

"What? That we had a bargain? That this engagement was all trumped up?"

"No." I held her by the shoulders, but gently, because I was frustrated but still felt so tender about her. "I would tell them that you're hot and cold. That it makes me crazy. That I can't read you, and I can't figure you out. That one minute you are all over me and the next you push me away. That I want you so badly, and I love the way you are, but that I find you totally absolutely crazy-making at the same time. And that makes me want to just push you out of my life."

"So push me out," she said, challenging me.

"Yeah? That's what you want?"

"Absolutely," she said in that crisp, too-controlling voice. "Just push me out. I'll be on my way, and you'll be on your way, and it'll be all fine, as if this week never happened. We'll both get what we want."

"Will we?" I asked, moving in closer to her. "Will we get what we want?"

"Yes, of course. And then you can go, like you want to."

"What if I don't want to?" We were so close now, I could almost see the waves of emotion radiating from her tense, tight body.

"What do you want then, Reeve? What could you possibly want?"

"What if I want you?"

She closed her eyes briefly, and I wished I knew what she was thinking. I wished I had the secret code to her heart, like I had to her body. "You don't though," she said in a resigned voice. "You don't want me."

"I do," I said roughly, gripping her arm. Then I loosened my hold on her, but still held her close. She was shaking the tiniest bit, and I worried that I'd scared her. "Sutton," I said, lowering my voice, "you make me crazy, and I want you. I totally want you. So much. In every way. Every real way."

I dropped a hand to her waist, and felt her move toward my touch.

"You do?"

I nodded. "I do."

"For real?" she asked, and her voice wavered.

I wanted to hold her and reassure her, so I placed a hand gently on her cheek and looked in her eyes. "Those kisses? They were not fake. I promise. And this? Right now," I said, stopping to brush my lips against hers, so softly, so gently, I heard her gasp. "Not an act, either."

"Reeve," she said. "I'm not pretending with you. I'm not pretending at all."

"Neither am I." I ran my hands along her sides, over the fabric of her dress, feeling the heat from her body. "And this, right now? This is real. When I turn you around and lift up your dress, when I slide into you—that won't be an act. But I'll only do it if you say yes to me, Sutton."

She looked up at me, and she was soft and vulnerable. She was the Sutton who liked books, the Sutton who let herself be saved, the Sutton who wanted to know who I really was. She was the woman I'd loved getting to know better this crazy, topsy-turvy week.

"We can't do it here," she whispered.

There it was. An entrée. "I spotted a guest bedroom right by the cellar. Unoccupied."

"Oh God," she gasped as if astonished she was agreeing.

Good. All I wanted was exactly what I said at the table—I wanted her yes.

We left the cellar, ducked into the pristine bedroom, shut and locked the door.

Then she turned around, placed her hands against the wall. I hiked her skirt up to her hips and slid a hand between her legs, rewarded with my favorite thing in the world—how ready she was for me. Her panties were damp, and as I touched the cotton panel between her legs, I could feel the wetness all the way through. I reached inside my wallet, took out a condom, opened it, and put the wrapper back into my pocket. I unzipped the pants she'd bought for me, lowered my boxer briefs, and rolled on the condom. Like her, I was more than ready. I was aching to be inside her. Deftly, I drew her panties down to her knees, and angled her hips up slightly. She arched back, an invitation. I slid two fingers across her and she breathed out hard at my touch. Her body was trembling—she wanted this so much. She wanted me so much. As I glided my fingers against her, I knew exactly how ready she was for me. God, she needed it, she needed me so badly right now, just as much as I needed her. I stroked her more, grinning as she gasped and leaned her head back. She was so turned on, and that made me even harder.

I pushed against her wetness, groaning as I began to enter her. She was silky and soft and tight, and soon I filled her up, pausing to savor the absolute fantastic feeling of being inside her. Inside this woman I wanted, a woman I adored.

"Does this feel good?" I asked in a soft voice.

"It's incredible. I love it."

I rocked into her. "How much do you love it?"

"I'm so turned on," she murmured.

"More than you've ever been before?" I asked as I slid almost all the way out, making her moan.

"I've never wanted anyone this much."

I stayed like that, teasing her, knowing how risky it was to be playing like this at someone's house. But I didn't care. I didn't care one bit about what they thought.

"Are you sure?" I asked, rocking an inch into her, but no more. She shivered and tried to push back onto me. But I held tight to her hips.

"Yes, God yes."

"Say *please*, then, Sutton. Say please."

She trembled in my arms, glanced behind me, her eyes blazing with desire. "Please."

I thrust deep into her, and she said my name in a hot whisper.

I drove into her, feeling her tighten around me.

With one hand holding her hip, I moved my other hand around to the front, touching her where she needed it most. She grabbed my wrist instantly, adjusting the rhythm of my hand.

Her ownership of her pleasure sent a fresh wave of lust crashing over me. "You like that?"

"Yes," she said, in a raspy voice.

"Should I stop, then?" I teased her.

"No," she said, her voice worried. "Please don't stop."

"Are you sure?" I asked as I moved in and out of her.

"I'm begging you. I'm begging you not to stop."

"Just this once, then." I kept up the motions, rocking into her glorious wetness and touching her, my body pressed against her, feeling as if I were surrounding her, with pleasure, with sensations, with the purity of the absolute and perfect chemistry that existed between the two of us. I loved that she couldn't control this, that she didn't want to turn it off, that cool and calm Sutton was far out of her reach. She was hot and wild Sutton. She was needy Sutton. She was burning, fiery Sutton whose body cried out for me to bring her to the wildest and fiercest of places—to that far edge of want.

With one final thrust, and one slide of my fingers, she gasped, shuddered, and came so hard on me that I could literally feel the intensity of her orgasm spread throughout her body, and that was all it took for me to finish off too.

22

SUTTON

Reeve and I decided we should go back one at a time, using a stop at the loo for an excuse for taking so long. I went first, quietly opening the door and slipping out of the bedroom, straightening my skirt as I turned—

And found Janelle sitting at one of the barstools at the lounge, kicking the foot of her crossed leg and still managing to look uptight.

Or maybe that was because I shrieked in surprise.

Reeve came charging out of the bedroom to my rescue. I gave him a horrified look to make sure he was entirely dressed and zipped—and he was. Not that we fooled Janelle, obviously.

"Heavens, it took you long enough," she said.

In spite of everything on the line, I couldn't control my expression or the way my posture became straight enough to rival hers. "I beg your pardon?"

Janelle raised a brow. "To get the wine, dear. What else would I mean?"

"I . . ." How on earth did one broach the subject? What could I possibly say? I'm sorry, and I hope this won't affect our working relationship, but were you spying on my fiancé and me having sex just now?

Not bloody likely.

"Only you've not actually brought out any wine," Janelle pointed out.

I looked from my hands to Reeve's as if a bottle might materialize, but none did.

"I suppose I'll just get it myself." She uncrossed her legs to get down from the stool and Reeve said, "No, wait! I'll get it."

He went into the cellar and Janelle came over to me and whispered like we were girls at a slumber party, "You were right. I did not mean to get the bottle of wine."

I was sure all the blood drained from my face. "You didn't?"

"I mean that the chemistry between you is incendiary, and you can't keep your hands off each other. I have been giving the pair of you every opportunity to get together."

Oh my God, what was I going to do? Could I work for this woman knowing I had sex in her penthouse during her dinner party? Could I work with her thinking she might have watched us? Or at least engineered it in her own way?

All right, Sutton. You just have to do what you would do in any other situation. Cut to the chase.

"Janelle . . ." I cleared my throat then womaned up to handle this before Reeve came out. "Did you . . .?"

That was as far as I got.

"Oh dear God, no. I have quite enough sexual power plays to deal with vis-à-vis my husband. I had just hoped that you would seal the deal with Reeve—if you take my meaning, and I think you do—before you sign the contract with Pinkerton."

"Because it's . . . contingent on my being engaged?"

"Not at all, because once it's a binding agreement I have no more leverage over Johnathan, and he doesn't approve of my little matchmaking games."

I hadn't heard Reeve come out of the cellar, but I saw her gaze flick his way. She usually smiled—sort of —when she saw him, but this time her lips tightened into the frown version of her singular expression. "You are adorable together, so much so that I didn't even care that you, Sutton, outright lied about being engaged. I came to your office to tell you I knew, but then I met Reeve and, well, frankly the only thing I was interested in watching was how you were going to try to pull this off.

"It's been wildly entertaining, my dears, but tonight Johnathan will offer you the contract, Sutton. And as for you, you handsome young thing," Janelle said to Reeve, closing the distance and walking her fingers up his arm without actually touching him. "If Johnathan knows what's good for him—and he does, because I will tell him—you will have an audition." Now the finger waggled. "No guarantees . . ." She gave him a wink that could be seen from the space station. "But I have been very impressed with your acting and could easily see you in *Escorted Lives*."

* * *

I had never seen Reeve so elated. So emotional. He ordered another round of drinks at Dahlia's, the bar where we'd gone to celebrate. I always had a hunch I'd win the job casting the production, but it was a bigger gamble that he'd win a role. Our bargain was only that he get a chance to audition. I couldn't guarantee him a part even if it weren't against my ethics. But Janelle was married to the money, so she could. Janelle hadn't specified *which* part, but it was what a hungry actor wanted more than anything—an opportunity.

Reeve had been down on his luck, and now he was on top of the world, glowing like a little boy on Christmas morning. I'd seen that look on many handsome young men, and enjoyed being the one to put it there with good news.

"We pulled it off, Sutton! We pulled it off, babe." He pumped a fist in victory, then laughed giddily. "And not to say I told you so, but I had a feeling that woman was up to something. Matchmaking in her own way and a bit of a peeping tom. Isn't that crazy?"

"Totally." I smiled. Janelle was an odd one, but every woman was entitled to her own kink.

Reeve grabbed me and kissed me hard on the mouth, and I gave in for a moment to the feel of him. When he ended the kiss, he pounded his fist on the bar and shouted, "Best night of my life."

It was a very good night for me too. That was true. But yet, he hadn't said anything more about the two of us. I'd admitted in the wine closet that I wasn't pretending, that I had real feelings for him. Wouldn't now be the perfect moment for us to figure out what was next? Would we spend more time together? But as the night wore on, Reeve never mentioned where we would go from here.

He was still in his celebratory mood, happy and toasting everyone and everything. Except for us.

It was a different side of him. I'd call him anything but grumpy, but this outright joy was lovely to watch, and it should be contagious. It was so unequivocally genuine. But that was the problem. He was unquestionably *not* acting, and my certainty about that made me uncertain about . . . everything else.

Suddenly, I had a horrible headache and had to go home.

* * *

Alone with my dog, I wrote to my friend.

Sutton: Have you ever gotten what you wanted and been kind of a selfish malcontent about it because it's a cherry short of a perfect sundae?

McKenna: Oh, honey. I live in California. That's a Tuesday for people here.

Sutton: Well, I'm unhappy about feeling unhappy.

McKenna: Spill. Because my shovel is still yours if you need it.

Sutton: Remember I said I'd fallen in like with Reeve? Well . . . tonight I sort of fell into sex with Reeve.

McKenna: I'm not even going to ask how that can happen. I want to know what you're going to do about it.

Sutton: Nothing.

McKenna: WHERE IS SUTTON? PUT HER BACK ON THE PHONE.

Sutton: No, really. Reeve kept his eye on the prize, and he's thrilled just to have an audition, and I think I just let what I wanted to see fill in gaps of what was there. And then all the emotion, and we just—what I said.

McKenna: Sutton. My sweet cinnamon roll. No one is that good an actor. He could be the clone of Laurence Freaking Olivier, but you are a professional. It's your job to tell how well actors can act.

Sutton: That doesn't mean anything if I didn't pay attention. If I got caught up in how I felt, and the one thing I DO know is real, which is that we have massive chemistry.
But desire isn't the same thing as . . . more than like.

McKenna: Desire isn't the same thing as falling in like for some people. But it is for you. You like Reeve, and the only way you'll find out if he sees something worth going for is if you talk to him.

Sutton: Why do I love you so much for telling me things I don't want to hear?

I didn't understand why Sutton wasn't happy. Ecstatic, even. She got the gig she wanted, and we were both open about liking each other, right? Also, we had mind-blowing sex. Life should be good.

So why wasn't she returning my calls or texts? Why was I at Jill's apartment playing Scrabble when I wanted to be with Sutton?

I stared at my letter tiles, not really seeing them. It was Sunday afternoon, two days after the most epic sex and most epic night of my life, and I was playing Scrabble with Jill and her roommate Kat, three people with social lives as scrambled as the letter tiles in the box lid.

Scrabble was a favor for Jill, who had the audition of her life coming up and couldn't relax. I didn't even like the game, but I understood that kind of anxiety, so Scrabble it was.

"Jihad!" Kat declared as she placed four tiles around an "h."

Groaning loudly, Jill flopped back on to the couch as Kat counted up her points. "That's a triple letter for J and a double word score, so add it up, babies. Add. It. Up. That is 64 points for moi. Plus, an excellent and not overused word."

"There are no extra points for quality of the word, just the letters," Jill said, sitting back up and stretching. "What I do need, though, is a quality coffee. Let's go down to the bodega."

Kat made a face. "I thought you said quality coffee. If I'm leaving the house, then I insist we go someplace with macchiatos."

"Works for me." She climbed to her feet. "You good with that plan, Reeve?"

I was staring into space again—it had happened a lot this weekend—but shook my head and got to my feet too. "Thanks, but no. I need to get going."

Jill looked like she would say something—call out how I hadn't even bothered to come up with a good lie, or maybe just ask me—again—how I was doing. But Kat nudged her toward the door.

"Let's all be off, then," she said in a jaunty voice. I supposed a sixty-four-point word entitles a person to be jaunty.

We went separate ways, Jill and Kat toward the coffee shop, and me in whatever direction they weren't going. My idle path took me to the Lucky Spot, and I ducked inside. I hadn't realized when I turned down coffee it was because I'd really wanted something stronger. But if I'd had, I might have helped myself to whatever alcohol was in the Chelsea apartment and this was better. Among other things, Spencer was behind the bar.

"So," I said, sliding onto a barstool. "Think the Yankees have a shot next year?"

Spencer put a highball glass on the bar and gestured to the liquor shelves. "What'll it be? Alcohol is a more reliable social lubricant than talking about sports. You don't have to pick a side to be on."

"Yeah, you don't have to pick a team to root for, and you can switch whenever you want." I asked for what I wanted, Spencer poured it, and pushed the glass in front of me.

He went to work wiping down the bar. "You going to talk about what's actually wrong, or do we wait until the alcohol kicks in?"

"So, you're not even going to pretend I'm here just for the booze?"

"You're in a bar on a Sunday afternoon. So is it work trouble, car trouble, or romantic trouble?"

I sighed. "The last one."

"Ah," Spencer said. "So, you didn't come here just to look at my pretty face." He made a bring it on motion. "Spill."

I kept it simple as I sipped my drink, never mentioning Sutton by name. "She's hot and cold, and I don't know why. But I think it's because she doesn't know or doesn't believe I'm really into her. It's this weird thing with actors. It's like, sometimes the people you go out with never really trust you because they always think you're acting."

"That kind of sucks," Spencer said.

"Yeah."

"But, *are* you into her?" he asked.

"Hell yeah."

He wiped an invisible spot from the bar near me. "Then the answer is clear. You have to let her know."

"I thought I had." My shoulders slumped and I leaned over my drink. A complete sad sack, that was me.

"Maybe you thought you had, but if she's not sure, make it clear," Spencer said. He was emphatic, the way someone can be when they speak from experience. "Trust me on this. When I realized Charlotte was the one for me, I had to do something drastic."

"What did you do?" I asked. I was an actor with limited resources for extravagant gestures.

"Laid it all out there for her. Told her exactly how I felt. That I'd fallen so damn hard for her and I couldn't stand the thought of her being out of my life."

"And it worked?" I didn't know if things could be that simple.

"I'll let you know when we get to our next anniversary."

I raised my glass in a wordless toast.

"So listen," Spencer said earnestly, "whether you love this chick or just like her, you need to make it abundantly clear. Put your heart on a goddamn platter and give her the choice to be with you."

I stood up and reached for my wallet, putting some bills on the bar. "You are a steely-eyed missile man. Or a wise man. Or Yoda. Or something. I'm gonna go find her."

"One more thing," he said, taking my payment to the till. "Don't show up empty-handed. Bring her a gift. But not flowers or chocolate. Get her something that matters to her."

Something that matters to her.

I knew exactly what that was.

24

REEVE

"Is this going to fit?"

I held up the sweater thing and asked the saleswoman.

She nodded. "Yes, for that size and weight. It'll be a perfect fit."

"Okay. Can you wrap it? But nothing too girly. Maybe just a black bow or something?"

The saleswoman nodded, and minutes later she handed me the gift. I paid for it, thanked her, and ran the few blocks from the Madison Avenue shop to Sutton's apartment building. I buzzed once and waited. There was no answer. I called her. She didn't pick up her phone. Damn, this was going to hell quickly. So much for my big gesture. I looked down at the gift. Was it even the right big gesture?

I buzzed once more, but was met with silence.

"Come along, darling. Let's go home and have some dinner."

I smiled to myself at the sound of her voice, then

turned around. She was looking the other way as The Artful Dodger sniffed a bush. She looked adorable in her jeans and pullover jacket. She had a scarf around her neck, and her hair was down. I loved her hair. I wanted to bury my face in her hair, and run my fingers through those beautiful strands.

I ran down the steps and stopped in front of her.

"Oh." She seemed taken aback to see me.

"Hi."

She tried to rein in a smile. It was like she was rearranging her expression. It was adorable and I loved it. "Hello."

"How are you?"

Then she returned to in-control Sutton. "I'm great. How are you? Are you so excited about the movie? I bet your agent is thrilled. I'm so proud of you. I knew you could do it."

I placed a hand on her arm. "You're babbling. You're making small talk. You're chatting about business. I'm not here for business reasons. I'm here on personal reasons," I said and smiled at her. I hoped she knew the smile was for her. That it was for real. But hoping and wishing wouldn't be enough.

"Sutton, I stand by what I said in the wine closet. You are the most stubborn and complicated woman I have ever known. But I also want to get to know you. I want to know the real you. I want to walk your dog with you and find out how you drink your coffee, and I want to see what you look like in the morning, and even if you think you don't look hot in the mornings, I already know you're wrong because you are always hot to me. I said yes to the job because I had a thing for you. I had a crush on you. And then I spent a week with you, and now I have a hell of a lot more than a crush on you."

I watched her as her features softened, as her hard shell started to break. "What do you mean more than a crush?"

I rolled my eyes. "Sutton Brenner, I. LIKE. YOU. Okay? Not like fake fiancé like. Not like pretend boyfriend like. Not like an actor-trying-to-get-a-role like. I have fallen into mad like with you. And I have no idea if you like me back, okay? You needed something from me and yet it's like you doubted me every step of the way, and I could be making a complete ass of myself and reading everything wrong, and maybe it was only one way. Maybe it was only me for you. But if you like me at all too, then let's just see what happens when we're not trying to get something."

Sutton muttered something in a small voice.

I shook my head. "I didn't hear you."

"I'm sorry I was difficult. I'm sorry I was infuriating. I'm sorry I was hot and cold."

"It's okay," I said and moved closer to her. I glanced down and saw The Artful Dodger wagging his tail. "Your dog looks happy."

"He's always happy," Sutton said with a smile. "He's also especially happy when I'm happy."

"Are you then? Happy?"

"I like you too," she said, and I knew how hard it was for her to say those words.

My lips curved into a grin. "For real?"

"For real. So for real it's like beyond real," she said, unable to stop smiling too. "I like you almost as much as I like my dog."

I wrapped her in an embrace. "Now that's saying a lot. And speaking of, I got him a gift."

25

SUTTON

My fingers became thumbs as I nervously undid the ribbon. My heart fluttered, and my body sang, and I felt so foolish for having doubted him. I'd been falling for my actor boy, falling so hard I'd feared how much it would hurt. Now he was here, and he had a gift for my dog. I held The Artful Dodger's leash tightly in one hand as I opened the box.

I gasped when I saw what was inside. A perfect navy-blue fleece coat for the winter months. I pulled it out quickly. "It's the perfect size for him! How did you know his size?"

Reeve shrugged. "Told you I was good with sizes. I took a wild guess that he was about nine pounds. Was I right?"

"He's exactly nine pounds! You got my dog a gift," I said, and maybe it seemed small, and maybe it seemed silly, but the fact was Reeve knew the way to my heart was through my dog. "I can't wait to put it on him. Let's get rid of this old ratty coat and take him for a walk in his new one." Then I stopped talking and my nerves came back. "That is, if you want to."

"Sutton Brenner, I went into a *dog accessory shop* on *Madison Avenue*. Yes, I want to walk your dog with you. But there's also something I want you to do for me."

"Yes?"

"I want you to ask me to spend the night with you, and I want you to let me stay over."

I blushed. My hesitation had nothing to do with reluctance and everything to do with savoring this moment. "Reeve, will you spend the night with me?"

His smile lit up my heart. It was mine. *He* was mine.

* * *

After we shed our jackets and shoes, I took his hand, threaded my fingers through it, and led him to my room. I took off my shirt, my pants, my knickers.

Well, that's not precisely true.

He took off my knickers.

And he seemed to savor every moment of the undressing.

I trembled as he removed that last item of clothes, then as he regarded me. "You're beautiful," he said, and he looped an arm around my waist. "And you're mine now."

I thrilled at the possessiveness, loving the way he wanted to claim me with his words, with his touch.

But there was the little problem of his lack of nudity.

I tap-danced my fingers along his chest. "You're mine too, but I like you in your birthday suit."

He wiggled his brows. "Then you can have me that way. And then you can have your way with me."

He stripped off his clothes, took me to bed, and covered me with kisses, layering soft, sweet kisses on my neck, my breasts, my belly. I shivered from his touch, closing my eyes.

Someone else was enjoying the moment too, because when I opened my eyes, my little darling—the four-legged one—was sitting on the pillow, wagging his tail, watching.

Reeve laughed. "Someone's a little pervert."

"He's absolutely a perv," I said with a grin. "But he's a well-trained one." I pointed to the floor, "Down, love."

The Artful Dodger shot me a profoundly sulky look but did as he was told.

Then it was just me and Reeve, this wonderful man. This charming, dirty, vulnerable, sweet, and rough man I'd fallen for.

His hands traveled up my body. His lips brushed kisses over me, and I felt cherished.

I felt adored.

And I felt us both falling into each other.

Soon our kisses and our touches turned heated, and he reached for a condom. Before he rolled it on, though, I set a hand on his chest. "I'm clean and on protection."

"I'm clean too," he said, and then he spread my legs, positioned himself between them, and sank inside.

I moaned from the sheer pleasure, from the utter intensity, and from the unexpected *newness*.

This wasn't our first time.

But in a way it was.

He looked at me like it was.

And when he whispered, "Hi, beautiful," I felt that it, too, was a first.

The first time he'd made love to me.

That's what it was as we moved together, tangled up in each other, arms, legs, sweat, heat, and breath.

Soon, we were both panting, gasping, moaning each other's name and falling over the edge.

After, as we lay there sated, I took another leap. I kissed his cheek and whispered what was completely real. "It's not just like. I'm falling for my fake fiancé."

He smiled, kissed my nose, and whispered, "It's so much more than like. I'm falling for my girlfriend."

That's what I was now.

That's what I wanted to be.

He nodded and leaned in to brush his lips against mine, and it felt so good. It felt right. It felt real.

EPILOGUE

Reeve

Present Day

The metal dug into my wrists. The bright lights shone on me. I was handcuffed to the bedpost on set, wearing only my boxer briefs and cowboy boots. Because that's what the script dictated the lead actor in *Escorted Lives* should wear in this scene. And I had not only won a part, as Janelle had promised, I'd won the starring role.

"Tell me when it hurts," the actress playing opposite me said.

"Doesn't hurt," I said.

Her hands wrapped around me, tugging on each end of the handcuffs, tightening them. I felt another pair of hands slide up my back. I sucked in a breath. I could have acted. I could have pretended it didn't feel great when Sutton Brenner touched me. But it did, it had, and it probably always would. Even now, five months later, five months into our real relationship, everything with her was amazing, right down to the real ring I'd bought for just the right moment. We'd fallen fast into real like during that one week, and even faster into real love in the months that followed.

But she wasn't acting in the film with me, so she stepped back to take her post with the crew and watch the pivotal scene as the leading client had her way with her male escort. Everyone had their thing, in film and in real life.

Sutton and I had ours. We'd done plenty of wild things in our time together, but my favorite—and Sutton's too—was when I asked her to beg for it. She always did, and I always made sure she was rewarded.

Then we'd fall asleep together, and wake up together, and go to dinner and the movies and dog walks together, and every real second with her was as excellent as every pretend second had been.

Better, actually.

But for now, I put Sutton and our times out of my mind. I had a role to play. A job to do. I was an actor, and I gave it my all as the camera started to roll.

ANOTHER EPILOGUE

Reeve

A little later

I pulled out a green slatted chair from the round table and waited for my woman to sit in it. She did, crossing her sexy legs.

I bent closer to her ear. "Love this view," I said, then brushed my hand up her arm and along her collarbone. She murmured, and I enjoyed the sound of her desire.

But there would be time later to stoke fires and put them out in the best way possible.

I took a seat across from her at the Sunshine Bakery. The night of the Pinkerton's dinner, I'd told her I'd take her here. It might have been a small thing, but I wanted Sutton to know I was a man of my word, so we'd gone together and had been many times since.

She slid the yellow plate closer to me. "Your heart's desire. A grapefruit macaron."

My stomach rumbled. I did indeed love grapefruit in all its forms. I picked up the treat and popped it in my mouth. I moaned in delight. "It tastes like citrus and sunshine and sweetness."

Sutton grinned happily. "You need to tell Josie how much you love it." She gestured to the bakery counter, where the woman who owned this shop worked. But the brunette was occupied chatting with a man at the counter.

But I only had eyes for Sutton. I had the ring I'd gotten her, the one that came with a very particular question, in my pocket, waiting for me to decide on the perfect moment.

But there is no perfect moment. There was this moment, though, and I wanted to grab it so that it never became a lost moment.

"It was delicious," I told Sutton. "But that's not my heart's desire."

Something in my expression must have given something up. It seemed ridiculous that she had ever worried about the truth of my feelings, when I could hide nothing from her.

"It's not?" she asked.

"Nope."

"Italian food, then?"

"Not that, either." I slid forward in my seat and took the ring box out of my pocket. "It's a brilliant leggy brunette who I want in my life forever."

She covered her mouth with her hands and tears brimmed on her lashes. "Reeve . . . Truly?"

"I would never lie to you."

The next moment we were on our feet, then I swept her off hers and into my arms. There was laughing and crying, and then Josie and her guy in scrubs realized there was something going on and there was more laughter, more tears—but happy ones, all of them.

Happy and bright and sweet like a grapefruit macaron.

THE END

Curious about Sutton's friend McKenna? Dive into her fun, fresh, sexy fake fiancé romance THE DATING PROPOSAL, available everywhere.

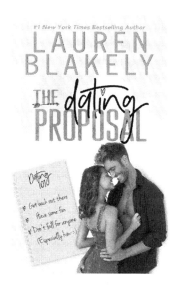

How about Chase and Josie? What's the story with their crazy chemistry and flirty glances? Find out in FULL PACKAGE, a sexy, hilarious friends-to-lovers romance. FULL PACKAGE is a full-length rom-com and it is available everywhere! Sign up for my newsletter to receive an alert when these sexy new books are available.

ALSO BY LAUREN BLAKELY

Big Rock Series

Big Rock

Mister O

Well Hung

Full Package

Joy Ride

Hard Wood

The Gift Series

The Engagement Gift

The Virgin Gift

The Decadent Gift (coming soon)

The Heartbreakers Series

Once Upon a Real Good Time

Once Upon a Sure Thing

Once Upon a Wild Fling

Boyfriend Material

Asking For a Friend

Sex and Other Shiny Objects

One Night Stand-In

Lucky In Love Series

Best Laid Plans

The Feel Good Factor

Nobody Does It Better

Unzipped

Always Satisfied Series

Satisfaction Guaranteed

Instant Gratification

Overnight Service

Never Have I Ever

Special Delivery

The Sexy Suit Series

Lucky Suit

Birthday Suit

From Paris With Love

Wanderlust

Part-Time Lover

One Love Series

The Sexy One

The Only One

The Hot One

The Knocked Up Plan

Come As You Are

Sports Romance

Most Valuable Playboy

Most Likely to Score

Standalones

Stud Finder

The V Card

The Real Deal

Unbreak My Heart

The Break-Up Album

21 Stolen Kisses

Out of Bounds

The Caught Up in Love Series:

The Swoony New Reboot of the Contemporary Romance Series

The Pretending Plot (previously called *Pretending He's Mine*)

The Dating Proposal

The Second Chance Plan (previously called *Caught Up In Us*)

The Private Rehearsal (previously called *Playing With Her Heart*)

Stars In Their Eyes Duet

My Charming Rival

My Sexy Rival

The No Regrets Series

The Thrill of It

The Start of Us

Every Second With You

The Seductive Nights Series

First Night (Julia and Clay, prequel novella)

Night After Night (Julia and Clay, book one)

After This Night (Julia and Clay, book two)

One More Night (Julia and Clay, book three)

A Wildly Seductive Night (Julia and Clay novella, book 3.5)

The Joy Delivered Duet

Nights With Him (A standalone novel about Michelle and Jack)

Forbidden Nights (A standalone novel about Nate and Casey)

The Sinful Nights Series

Sweet Sinful Nights

Sinful Desire

Sinful Longing

Sinful Love

The Fighting Fire Series

Burn For Me (Smith and Jamie)

Melt for Him (Megan and Becker)

Consumed By You (Travis and Cara)

The Jewel Series

A two-book sexy contemporary romance series

The Sapphire Affair

The Sapphire Heist

CONTACT

I love hearing from readers! You can find me on
Twitter at LaurenBlakely3, Instagram at
LaurenBlakelyBooks, Facebook at
LaurenBlakelyBooks, or online at LaurenBlakely.com.
You can also email me at
laurenblakelybooks@gmail.com